UNRAVELLING ROANA

A REGENCY NOVELETTE

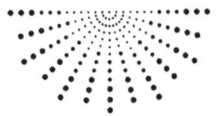

ROSIE CHAPEL

Unravelling Roana

Rosie Chapel

First printing: 2021
ISBN: 978-0-6451116-2-0 (e-book)
ISBN: 978-0-6451116-3-7 (paperback)

Ulfire Pty. Ltd.
P.O. Box 1481
South Perth
WA 6951
Australia

www.rosiechapel.com

Cover Designed by Rosie Chapel
Images Courtesy: Period Images and Deposit Photos (artist - qwerty 2013)

❀ Created with Vellum

There is something so different in Venice from any other place in the world, that you leave at once, all accustomed habits and everyday sights to enter an enchanted garden.

Mary Shelley

CHAPTER ONE

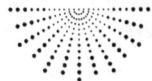

BROOKETON MANOR ~ AUGUST 1819

Gideon Dumont, 6th Earl of Brooketon, stared at the letter. The words made no sense. *Ro had left him?* He shook his head. Here was he rushing to their country estate, looking forward to spending what was left of the summer with his wife, only to find her missing, and no one seemed to know where she had gone.

How was this possible?

Where was she?

How could someone so vital, simply disappear?

He gripped the sheet and studied it for the fifth time.

Nothing had changed.

My darling, Gideon,

Darling! Am I entitled to call you that? You are to me. You always have been, and you always will be, so I shall grant myself one last indulgence.

If you are reading this, you know I am not at Brooketon

1

Manor. I do not expect you to forgive my flight, but I could not stay. The rumours, the whispers, the well-intentioned *comments have become untenable.*

I know many among our peers have affairs, kept under wraps, to scratch an itch their respective spouses seem unable to satisfy. I thought we were different. I thought we had a strong, loving marriage. I trusted, I hoped, I was enough.

Evidently, I was mistaken, and to think you found it necessary to seek another has broken me. I cannot stand by and watch the oaths we took disintegrate before my eyes.

For most of the last eight years we have been inseparable, yet I admit to being aware of a growing distance between us. Of late, you are never home and when you are, your mind is elsewhere. I can only presume, with her.

I miss sitting with you at the end of the day, engaging in lively conversation, or reading together. I miss taking constitutionals through one of the parks, or an exhilarating ride along Rotten Row. I miss your touch. Oh Gideon, I just miss you.

How tedious — a wife who wants to be with her husband.

Doubtless, I should be grateful for the brief happiness we shared — yes, eight years out of what I believed would be forever, is brief — but I am not. I am angry, hurt, disillusioned and betrayed.

If I was so lacking as a wife, why did you not talk to me? Legally, we are bound for life, but I am unable to live with your indifference.

In order to retain a shred of dignity, I have taken control of my destiny. Rather than air our problems in public, to the glee of the ton, I have let it be known I am wearied of city life and am retiring to the country for the foreseeable future.

Mayhap our separation will provide you the space and time to decide what or who you want. The fetters you obviously abhor no longer confining you.

Thank you for being the adoring husband you once were. I love you and will treasure the memory of what we shared.

Roana

The letter had an ominous finality to it. *Him... indifferent? Never! What was all this nonsense about affairs and fetters? Where the devil was she?* Admittedly, his arrival had been delayed by circumstances beyond his control, but this...?

With a muffled roar, Gideon flung the page on the desk, and stormed through the rambling old house to the domestic quarters. He burst through the baize door and down the corridor to the kitchens.

The staff, snatching a moment's peace to eat a meal, shot to their feet.

"M-my lord," Chambers, the butler, stammered. "How may I, we, be of service?"

The rest waited, nervously. All knew Lady Brooketon had departed. One was privy to the reason, and she was sworn to secrecy.

"Where is my wife?" Gideon barked the question, his face thunderous.

"I am afraid I have no idea." Chambers replied, his tone sincere. "She asked that only one small trunk and her valise be packed. She left about three weeks ago."

"Three weeks?" Gideon's mouth fell open in shock. "And none of you thought to apprise me of this?"

"We thought her ladyship had returned to London."

An understandable assumption given the earl's conspicuous absence from the Manor.

London could be stifling in the summer, and it was customary for members of the *ton* to escape to their country estates for the duration of the hot weather. Nestled in rural Dorsetshire, Brooketon Manor was a haven. At the beginning of August, every year for the past eight years, Gideon brought Roana here and, invariably, the couple stayed until the end of September.

In early July, when their mistress arrived on her own, the staff had been disquieted. Not entirely convinced by her assurances, his lordship would follow in a month as was their habit. For them to travel separately was unprecedented. Moreover, Lady Brooketon seemed unusually withdrawn and agitated.

A little over three weeks past, to their well-concealed astonishment, her ladyship had requested the carriage be prepared. Until the earl's unexpected arrival earlier that day, they presumed she was with him in the capital.

"Who drove her?"

"I took Lady Brooketon as far as Winchester. She bade me return, insisting she wanted to continue on to London by mail coach." Drake, the groom, piped up. Gideon's expression darkened — if that was possible — prompting Drake to add, "Forgive me, my lord. I did me darndest to persuade her, but her ladyship point blank refused."

Gideon was floored and, momentarily contemplated whether this was, in fact, a nightmare. One he hoped to God he would wake from imminently.

Where was she?

Even when not at the Manor, Roana was everywhere. In the carefully chosen furnishings, the whimsical touches, the light and colour. Before they wed it was a dreary place, somewhere Gideon rarely visited. Now they spent close to six months of every year here, spread around their responsibilities in the city.

He was on several parliamentary committees. Roana dedicated her days to all manner of causes. Her favourite was helping the archivists at the British Museum, cataloguing acquisitions. All were voluntary, but she was devoted to them.

A self-confessed bluestocking, Roana had never been comfortable or skilled at ladylike pastimes. She had mastered them, but the results ranged from passable to execrable. She preferred books, history, and the outdoors, to sewing, dancing, and singing, although she enjoyed listening to music.

These were the things Gideon loved about her and he *did* love her. Her accusation he was involved in a dalliance with another woman cut him to the quick. He had been faithful to Roana from the moment he clapped eyes on her. She beguiled him, with her flaming auburn hair, sparkling green eyes, and vibrant personality.

While he retraced his steps through the house in search of any hint as to Roana's whereabouts, he recalled how she ticked him off for teasing, and alleged he was in his cups the first time he told her she was beautiful. He had been unaware her family considered her unprepossessing and the least marriageable of her siblings.

He had met Roana when she ran into him, literally, while trying to avoid some elderly viscount who thought she would submit to his advances. Gideon implied he was her escort for the evening, effectively discouraging the ardent gentleman.

Roana thanked him and they fell to chatting. Gideon was entranced by Roana's intelligence and her wit. That, to him, she was the most ravishing woman he had ever seen, merely a bonus.

His family tried to dissuade Gideon's suit, hoping he might find a more suitable bride. Roana's... idiosyncrasies were well-known. The handsome young man who had recently turned four and twenty was considered very eligible. Roana, at barely ten and eight, would find another swain.

Gideon was not to be thwarted, and dedicated every spare moment to courting Roana who, it was obvious, returned his affection. Before long, he had persuaded Roana, his love for her was the forever kind. He was the second son of duke, an earl in his own right. She, the youngest daughter of an earl. Their match was, reluctantly, approved.

They were married three months later.

That was nearly nine years ago and, as Roana's letter stated, the couple had been inseparable ever since.

Now, believing he had betrayed her love, she had vanished into thin air.

CHAPTER TWO

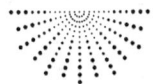

$\mathcal{F}$inding nothing of use downstairs, Gideon headed to their bedchamber. Upon entering, he surveyed the room carefully, his gaze alighting on the escritoire.

Propped against the lid was a sheet of paper. Carrying it to the window, he unfolded it and began to read.

My love,

His eyes closed. He felt the warmth of her touch as though she stood next to him, her hand on his chest.

I was resolved not to reveal my whereabouts to you. In my mind, you forfeited that right by breaking the pledge you made on our wedding day. Those wonderful vows you reiterated so often.

To my annoyance, my affection means, despite my anger, the notion I might cause you anxiety sits ill with me. Thus, I have devised a set of clues.

If you believe our love is worth fighting for, follow them and they will lead you to me.

Roana

. . .

A grudging smile curved his mouth. My, but she loved puzzles. Turning the sheet, he saw a crude drawing on the back. Peering at it, Gideon made out the letter T, and a simplistic outline of a boat next to what resembled a large blob. He twisted the paper this way and that, hoping a different perspective would help.

Stumped, he trudged back down to the kitchen. Perchance one of his staff might offer an opinion; anything was better than nothing. Half an hour, and a litany of hilarious suggestions later, Gideon was none the wiser.

The room fell quiet, then Molly, Roana's personal maid, who had not entered the discussion thus far, asked whether she might speak.

"Of course, Molly, I need all the help I can get. 'Tis clear Lady Brooketon had no mind to make this easy."

"I think I might know, but her ladyship swore me to secrecy." Molly dipped a low curtsy, her cheeks bright red. While loyal to her mistress, Molly hated seeing Lord Brooketon look so… devastated.

Gideon beckoned her forward and gentled his tones. "Lady Roana set me this clue and doubtless suspected I would come and ask. Please, Molly."

It was not done for an earl to plead with a member of staff, but Lord Brooketon was not your typical nobleman. He cared for those he employed here at the Manor and in London. He treated everyone with dignity and respect, as did Roana. These people who served them, who catered to their every need, were more family than their own flesh and blood.

Molly capitulated.

"Lady Brooketon told me about a voyage two people, them as who she works with at the museum, were about to

8

take. It was to..." Molly scoured her brain. Her face lit up when the destination popped into her head. "...Italy, that's it. Lady Brooketon *did* say it would be marvellous to learn more about something or other. Forgive me, Lord Brooketon. I forget what. I believe her colleagues had secured passage on a boat leaving from the Pool of London. I wondered mebbe, could that be what the drawing means? Mind, I do not know what T indicates."

Higgins, one of the footmen, pooh-poohed Molly's idea, but Gideon let it roll around his head.

A boat and a blob. The latter *could*, conceivably, be a puddle. It was entirely possible and gave him somewhere to start.

"Did she, by any chance, disclose when they were to depart?" he asked.

Molly shook her head. "No, my lord, but she was excited for them and, if you don't mind me saying, maybe a trifle sad not to be joining them."

"Thank you, Molly, you have been a great help. Higgins, have Fitz saddle Caesar, I must make haste." He waved aside the splutters from his staff about him leaving so soon, he had only just arrived, hadn't rested and so on. "I will partake of luncheon," he conceded, "but I want to be well on my way by dark."

With that he left them to their tasks.

His heart had begun to beat again.

Molly followed Gideon upstairs, ostensibly to assist with his repacking. In reality, she wanted to tell his lordship the rest.

"Beg pardon, my lord, there was one more thing."

She waited until Gideon gave her leave to continue, using the time to fold clothes neatly into his bag.

"Go on," Gideon nodded.

"I did not want to speak in front of the others. I am breaking her ladyship's confidence, but she said the reason she had to go was because of your affair with Lady de Beauvais." It was obvious Molly was uncomfortable repeating this, but she braved it out.

"*Lady de Beauvais?*" Gideon was stupefied. Roana was not one for standing idly by while something precious to her was threatened. Why had she not confronted either him or the lady in question?

"Her ladyship believed you preferred the marchioness and that was why you have been so cold." Swallowing her nerves, Molly made a determined effort to tell Gideon everything Roana had entrusted to her.

"Lady Brooketon said it was better to remove herself from the picture. She said as how her decision was aggr… agun…" Molly screwed up her face, battling with the unusual word, "augmented, that's it." Her look of relief would have been comical on any other occasion. "Augmented by the ongoing humiliation from those who took vindictive delight in salacious gossip, remarks from the marchioness herself and the evidence of her own eyes." With no little pride, she recited Roana's words verbatim and in a rush.

"Wait… you mean to say her ladyship witnessed me behaving inappropriately?" Gideon quizzed, his brow knitted in an attempt to recall how his wife had come to this conclusion.

Molly nodded.

"Did she elaborate?"

"No, my lord. Just that it was too painful to be a laughing-stock among the *ton.*"

"Thank you, Molly. I appreciate your candour. Please do not worry. The Lady Brooketon I know would doubtless anticipate this conversation. If it assuages your concern, I shall tell her I threatened to beat it out of you." He waggled his eyebrows theatrically, making Molly giggle.

She dipped another curtsy.

"Please find her, my lord. This 'ouse, it ain't the same without her." Blushing once again at her temerity.

"Fret not, Molly. I shall do my damnedest to locate her and will carry her back here over my shoulders if I have to." He grinned suddenly, his whole countenance lifting.

Molly smiled in response and fastened the straps on the leather bag. "All done, my lord."

"You're a good girl, Molly Bolam and don't let anyone tell you different." Gideon picked up his bag and followed the young maid down the stairs.

Back in the kitchen, he pulled a chair up to the scrubbed smooth table and proceeded to devour two slices of game pie washed down with a large cup of strong coffee.

"I do not know how long it will take me to find her. Rest assured, I shall, whereupon I will bring her home." Gideon stood to take his leave.

The smiles on the faces of those present, evidence as to how much his wife meant to them.

Moments later he was astride Caesar. The huge stallion thundered down the drive and, before long, they were on the London road.

CHAPTER THREE

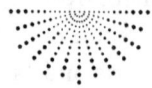

$\mathscr{F}$ar, far away, a slim gentleman of average height, leant on the rail of a boat, staring out at the horizon. They had been sailing for almost three weeks and all on board were looking forward to putting their feet on dry land again.

Their journey to date had been, blessedly, hazard-free and they had made good time thanks to favourable winds, although Captain Richards warned the Adriatic Sea had a tendency to be choppy.

The solitary passenger was joined by two older men. The trio chatted for a few moments, buffeted by the salty breeze, but the chill of the evening prompted them to seek their meagre quarters.

In the quiet of his cabin, the younger man removed his cap. Were any of the crew — bar the captain — watching, they would have been astonished to see a swathe of neatly plaited, rich auburn hair, tumble down his back. Longer than any cue a sailor would sport. Closer inspection revealed a pair of perceptive green eyes, a pert nose, and firm lips, set in a heart-shaped face.

Roana Dumont, Countess of Brooketon, had fooled all with her disguise. The captain knew, as did her companions, but to everyone else, she was plain Mr Dumont — although the crew *had* been heard to mutter, he seemed a bit foppish.

Maintaining the pretence was arduous, but no captain liked having an unescorted woman on board, married or single. It was only because Roana knew Lady Helena Drummond, that Captain Richards was persuaded to let her travel with them.

While Roana prepared for the evening, she let her mind wander over the last few weeks.

After dispatching Drake back to Brooketon Manor, Roana spent the night at the coaching inn where she effected a startling metamorphosis. The next day she obtained a seat on a mail coach to London. Thankfully, she was the only passenger and, dressed as a nobleman, her solitary status was not questioned.

Arriving in the capital, Roana's first mission was to secure suitable short-term lodgings. To stay at Dumont House was impossible. Gideon would be there.

She chose Mivart's, in the main because of their reputation for absolute discretion. The clerk raised a brow at Roana's claim she was Lord Parmenter — her maiden name — but he would never be so discourteous as to question a guest's identity.

Roana's next stop was the museum. She went straight to the office shared by her two colleagues who were due to depart in a matter of days. An hour later, she left, a bright smile on her face which had been unusually sombre of late.

From there, the countess headed to Stanton House, home of the Drummonds.

While not the hour for callers, Helena Drummond welcomed Roana with pleasure. Concealing her astonishment at the unexpected nature of the visit, not to mention her friend's peculiar garb, with remarkable aplomb.

"What a delightful surprise, and what luck we are still in London. We are headed to Whiteoaks by week's end." Helena greeted, referring to her family's country estate. "Come, let us go into the garden, it is more preferable to be outside than stuck in a stuffy parlour."

She tucked Roana's arm through hers and the two women strolled through cool hallways into the pretty garden at the side of the house. Once comfortable on the wrought iron bench, shaded from the heat of the summer sun by a leafy plane tree, they sat quietly for a moment or so enjoying the tranquillity.

"What's going on, Ro?" Helena pried gently. "You told me you were going to Brooketon for the summer. Here we are, less than a month later, you are back and dressed in, shall we say, a most unorthodox fashion." She twisted until she could study her friend. "Please tell me. You know I will help if I can."

Helena grasped Roana's hand, not unaware of her dilemma. Their affection for each other ran deep, and Roana had confided her suspicions when first they manifest.

"I wish to go away, right away, out of England. No…" when Helena looked as though she might interrupt, "…let me finish. Gideon behaves as though I am invisible. No matter what I do, he takes no notice or, mayhap, he finds it easier to ignore my attempts to discuss the situation. I can only assume, whatever supposedly captivated him about me has withered and he has not the courage to tell me.

"'Tis obvious, Constance de Beauvais has bewitched him, and I cannot summon up the will to fight. I know that makes me pathetic and defeatist, but I find I have lost the inclination to compete for the man I love. The woman is everything I am not. Elegant, sophisticated, and at ease in Society, not forgetting, she is also a wealthy widow.

"I daresay she is amused by his attention and he is flattered by hers. As neither bothered to consider my feelings while indulging in their affair, I am retaliating in kind."

Helena frowned. "My dear, are you certain Gideon has been unfaithful? It seems out of character. You two have always been so happy, so very... together. Since you shared your fears, I have taken the time to watch him when you attend society events. His eyes never leave you." The gnawing impression, Roana had completely misinterpreted her husband's apparent neglect, niggled.

"It seems incontrovertible, Helena. I saw them at the Canouvilles' Ball. He had his arm around her, and she was resting her head on his chest. A similar thing happened at the Gavestons' picnic. Does he think me blind, stupid? You have no idea..."

Roana's voice trailed off, and her shoulders sagged, which along with her pinched lips and pale face were the only outward signs of how profoundly she was distressed.

"Thus," she drew herself upright, "I am here to beg a favour."

Helena waited.

"I have a hankering to travel. To immerse myself in art and antiquity. To explore in a manner reminiscent of those who ventured on a Grand Tour, although on a much smaller scale. Herein lies my favour. Please ask Hugh whether I might be permitted to join his ship headed to Venice three days hence?" Roana had a lot riding on Hugh Drummond approving her request, not least a clue left at Brooketon Manor.

Confounded, Helena gaped at Roana. This was the last thing she expected to hear.

"Ro... you... cannot... but... how...?" She shook her head and tried again. *"Venice?"* The word delivered in a high-pitched squeak.

"Two of my colleagues are going. They have been afforded an opportunity not only to assist in the conservation of some artefacts, but also to study the techniques employed in art restoration. I have a little experience from my work at the museum and believe six months away from here might help heal my heart, as well as give Gideon the space he so obviously desires."

Roana faltered again, and she felt tears threatening. With supreme effort, she regained her composure and gripped Helena's hand. "Please, Helena, I realise 'tis a lot to ask, and am aware voyages are fraught with risk, but if I stay here nothing will change."

Helena stood and paced the garden. She was torn between wanting to bash Roana's and Gideon's heads together, or having one of her husband's friends drop Gideon in the Thames for his thoughtless conduct. Helena was not convinced the earl was guilty of anything other than incautious behaviour, but it was apparent, reasoning would have little effect on his countess.

Roana was no fool. Helena knew her friend would be wholly cognisant of the ramifications of such a decision, acknowledging she must be deeply upset even to consider so radical a course of action.

"Let me speak with Hugh..." Helena held up her palm, as Roana began to thank her. "He may refuse. Moreover, Captain Richards not long ago returned with *The Diligence*."

She named one of Trentams' schooners, badly damaged in a storm. "He may not want to tempt Fate by taking an unaccompanied woman on board his ship."

Roana nodded. Sailors were renowned for their superstitions and she had no alternative but to acquiesce. "Thank you in advance for trying." She smiled, although it did not reach her eyes.

The subject was dropped, and they talked of more cheerful things for the remainder of Roana's visit.

The next evening, Hugh Drummond called on Roana at Mivart's, to affirm Captain Richards had agreed to her request. *The Eurybia* would sail on the tide two days hence.

"Have you told Brooketon?" Hugh quizzed after providing this information. "I confess, your petition places me in an awkward position."

"Thank you, Hugh. I appreciate your generosity and, by the time I am safely out of harbour, Brooketon will be apprised, very definitely, of my intentions. You are most fortunate. Never take it for granted." She did not elaborate, but Hugh, enlightened by Helena, knew what troubled Roana. It did not take a genius to work out her inference.

"Safe travels."

Roana offered a wan smile and handed Hugh a letter. "Should my husband come looking, please would you be so kind as to give him this."

Hugh took the letter and studied the folded sheet briefly before tucking it into his jacket pocket. "I will." Bowing, he left.

That was nineteen days ago.

Finally, she was nearing her destination.

CHAPTER FOUR

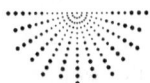

*B*efore long, Roana was settled in a relatively modest house in the district of Cannaregio. Here, grand palazzos and their aristocratic inhabitants rubbed shoulders with working-class neighbourhoods teeming with artisans and merchants.

Situated in the Campiello del Remer — off the Rio Terà Barba Frutariol, a minor canal — Roana's temporary abode, spread over four levels, came ready furnished. Although narrow, its numerous windows created an airiness, which, together with the tiled floors and light decor, kept the interior cool, even in the last of the summer heat.

Every day Roana, continuing to pose as a gentleman, attended the Royal Academy of Fine Arts along with Messrs Archibald and Brandisch — her colleagues from the British Museum.

Housed within the Scuola di Santa Maria della Carità, the academy was in the sestiere, or district, of Dorsoduro and not too far from her lodgings.

It took Roana no little time to master the unusual words, but the effort was worth it. The necessity of giving directions aside, Italian sounded so romantic.

In her quiet moments, Roana wished Gideon was there to share in the joy of discovery. He would be enthralled by Venice. The light, the colours, the hubbub, the aromas, the views… everything.

During her first week, whenever she had a free hour or so, Roana hired a gondola so she could admire the city from the Grand Canal. The architecture, seeming to blend that of Ancient Rome with Byzantine, evoked fairy tale castles. The combination, an artist's dream.

Occasionally, she alighted at Piazza San Marco to visit the impressive basilica or disembarked at the Rialto Bridge where she pottered around the adjacent, centuries old and famous market — the variety of stalls, astounding.

More often than not, she asked her gondolier to follow the Rio di Palazzo, passing beneath the exquisite Ponte dei Sospiri, the bridge connecting the Palazzo Ducale to the prison. According to the various books Roana had studied about the city, this bridge was the last thing prisoners saw before entering the gaol.

Nothing — not the books she read on the voyage, or the paintings she had seen in art galleries, not even the descriptions given by Captain Richards — prepared Roana for the veritable feast of the senses that was Venice. Despite being there for all the wrong reasons, she was very glad she had come.

Originally known as the Accademia di Belle Arti di Venezia, the Royal Academy of Fine Arts was founded in 1750. Quickly outgrowing its humble beginnings above a flour warehouse, the academy was relocated to the centuries old Scuola della Carità complex, itself subsequently transformed into the recently opened Galleria dell'Accademia.

Well over a quarter of a century previously, the academy had begun to study art restoration. Its popularity led to a comprehensive course in the subject being added to their curriculum.

This was one of the reasons Roana's colleagues were here. The knowledge they hoped to acquire would be vital for their continued success in the conservation and restoration of art and artefacts at the museum in London.

Roana, while interested in some of what the academy offered, also wanted to learn about Venice as a whole. The lectures were held each morning, leaving her free for the rest of the day. Determined to soak up every aspect of the city, Roana hired a bi-lingual guide, Marco, and used the after-noons to explore.

By the end of the third week, she had reached another decision. At Roana's request, Marco ferried her across the water to Murano, the tiny island where, once, glass factories abounded.

The glass blowers of Venice were renowned, their skill legendary, and she wanted to know whether one of the few remaining workshops might be willing to teach her.

Since the fall of the Venetian Republic a little over two decades previously, many of the methods employed to fabricate the exquisite glass were falling out of use. It would not take long for them to be forgotten.

Napoleon had ordered the factories be closed, effectively eliminating any competition between the Italian glassmakers and those in Austria and France. Nevertheless, the artisans were nothing if not tenacious, and pockets of industry survived.

Shortly after arriving in Venice, Roana had been privileged to visit a family-owned glass business. The stunning pieces on display touched something deep inside her.

Not one to be put off by the fact she was a woman — and no one knew that anyway — she prevailed upon Marco to set up a meeting. Napoleon's edicts had impelled the remaining glassmakers to become a secretive community, and the Pirozzi family required much persuading.

Roana was nothing if not determined and indicated, through Marco, she was prepared to pay handsomely for her tuition. Signore Pirozzi relented, remaining none the wiser this *Mr Dumont* was actually a countess.

On the agreed day, Roana had her first lesson in glass blowing.

England - August 1819

Given he didn't depart Brooketon Manor until early afternoon, Gideon made good time, relieved to see the skyline of London not quite three days after setting off.

Lonely hours in the saddle gave him plenty of time to think, and he had figured out what the 'T' stood for on Roana's drawing. Trentams. A shipyard owned by the Drummond family with whom they were close friends, especially Roana and Lady Helena Drummond.

Hugh Drummond and Gideon brushed shoulders through a covert government organisation for which they both worked. Had Gideon but known it, acquainting his wife — who was the soul of discretion — with even the minutest detail regarding his current assignment for said organisation, would have avoided this debacle.

The staff at Dumont House went into a spin when the earl turned up unannounced. Exhorting them not to fuss, Gideon assured them he intended staying only a few nights.

After a quick freshen up and change of clothes, he walked around to Stanton House. It was early evening, not the time to pay a call unless you were dining with the householder, but Gideon didn't care.

Rapping at the door, he was soon seated in the Drummonds' library sipping a fine Brandy and exchanging pleasantries with Hugh.

Fortuitously for Gideon, Helena — the only other person, in whom Roana confided — had just returned from Whiteoaks. Entering the library, she greeted Gideon with a hug, before punching him hard on his right shoulder.

"Ow, and good evening to you, Lady Helena." Gideon rubbed the maligned limb, his forehead creased in puzzlement.

"How *could* you?" She scowled, her violet eyes flashing with ire.

Gideon gaped at his hostess, momentarily confused. Light dawned, and his face cleared. "I am *not* having an affair with Lady de Beauvais."

"So, why does Ro think you are? She saw you together. Twice! Never mind the gossipmongers," Helena hissed.

Hugh and Gideon exchanged glances.

"Oh, no, please do not tell me you are part of this too?" She glared at her husband.

Hugh lifted his palm in conciliatory manner. "No, my love, but I know in what Gideon is involved."

"You, the pair of you, need to tell me what's going on this minute or the consequences will not be pretty." Her temper on the verge of spilling over, Helena jabbed her finger at the two men.

Hugh grinned at her fiery expression, not in the slightest perturbed by her outrage. "Perhaps you should sit, this might take some time."

The three made themselves comfortable, and Hugh began.

"We believe there are several new smuggling networks being established and we have been tasked with trying, either to infiltrate their gangs or track them down. In a nutshell, messages containing instructions, and bribes to guarantee silence, are being sent via coaching inns.

"We need to uncover from whom and where these are originating, without alerting the perpetrators. Three of our members have become highwaymen in an attempt to intercept any packages."

"Highwaymen? Is that not dangerous for them?" Helena interrupted.

Hugh nodded.

"It is, because they must act outside the law, but they are highly trained operatives and take every precaution. Lady de Beauvais has an estate south of Yarmouth, and another about thirty miles further north. Two areas seemingly targeted by the latest gang of smugglers," he elaborated, at Helena's raised eyebrow.

"The properties flow right down to the coast and we think the goods are being transported through her lands. Apparently, both estates are isolated. Their beaches easily accessible from sea and land. Perfectly positioned for smugglers."

"I understand that, but where does Gideon fit into this? Ro is not a simpleton. She witnessed Gideon embracing Constance. I fail to see how having an estate used by smugglers gives her the right to hug another woman's husband, not once but twice... and they are the occasions about which Ro knows." Helena made no effort to disguise her indignation or the implication there may have been other instances.

Gideon ran a hand through his dark hair and grimaced. "It was my fault. I was assigned to liaise with Lady de Beauvais because my presence would not be questioned. Simon de Beauvais and I were good friends. Before he died, he asked me not only to be one of his trustees, but also to keep a watchful eye on his wife, who remains unaware of this particular request."

"Why?"

"He feared she would fritter away his wealth with no thought for the children of his first marriage. Lady de Beauvais has a lavish lifestyle and does not like her extravagances to be curtailed."

"Surely their inheritance is protected?" Hugh interjected.

"The properties are, but not the coin."

"None of which explains why you were seen with her in your arms." Helena's patience was hanging by a thread.

"She appears to rely on me, to require my assistance in all manner of problems. I suspect 'tis a ruse to see whether I know more than I'm letting on or can be bribed. We have heard rumours, suggesting Lady de Beauvais is an active participant in the operation, allowing the smugglers to cross her lands unchecked for a tidy recompense.

"Thus, it works both ways — she unburdens herself more than she realises, and I am able to garner crucial intelligence we would otherwise miss."

"And tricking you into her bed. What was that? An added bonus?" Helena remarked wryly.

"She knows I am happily married," Gideon countered, heatedly.

"Since when has that ever stopped her? Even when Simon was alive, there were rumours. How do you suppose Roana felt when she saw the two of you together? Honestly, Gideon," Helena scoffed.

Gideon was about to reject Helena's assertions, when something gave him pause.

Scenes from recent balls and soirees floated through his mind.

His wife, politeness personified, behaving as expected, while her face remained devoid of expression. Their stilted conversations. Her obscure questions. Questions he had dismissed as inconsequential, so absorbed by his work he hardly registered what she asked him.

They had not been intimate for weeks, not even a kiss. For some couples in their circle this might be considered normal, for them it was unheard of.

Unbidden, Gideon recalled Roana coming into his study wearing a singularly diaphanous nightgown, trailing her fingers along his arm, brushing her lips to the nape of his neck.

Normally, this would be sufficient for him to drop everything and take her on his desk, but he had scarcely acknowledged her presence.

Now she had gone.

"Oh God, and Roana..." Gideon couldn't go on, as it

struck him what his wife suspected. How could he have been so obtuse? He lifted his head to stare at his friends, staggered by his insensitivity. "Helena, Hugh…"

Taking pity on him, Hugh reached into his jacket pocket and removed a sheet of paper.

"This might help." Before giving it to Gideon, he continued, "Be very sure, Gideon. To bring her back in order to save face is worse than the reason she fled in the first place."

CHAPTER FIVE

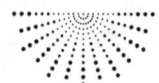

*G*ideon unfolded the sheet and scanned the words, then went back and read them again.

I am a city of islands
My pathways reflect the sky
My carriages do not need horses
Where am I?

He knew Roana was headed to Italy, that was all. His brain refused to comprehend her riddle. The director at the museum would know; he would pay him a call on the morrow. Gideon pinched the bridge of his nose. His head was beginning to ache, and he felt the sting of self-pity.

How could she do this to him?

Her face drifted through his mind again, and he forced aside his bruised ego. Ro was nothing if not a fighter. She would not have fled if she could see an alternative.

Inwardly, Gideon admitted to being surprised she had not confronted him. Then he remembered, a deep red stain colouring his cheeks. She had.

One afternoon, she had demanded an explanation for his behaviour. Other things crowding his mind, he had not given her question due regard. Without another word, she walked out.

The next day, she informed him she was leaving for their country estate.

Helena and Hugh observed the conflicting emotions chase across Gideon's face. They were quite prepared to tell him where Roana had gone, once convinced his reasons for following her were altruistic.

"Where the dickens is she, Drummond? You must know. She sailed on one of your ships."

Hugh's jaw dropped. "How on earth...?"

"This..." Gideon thrust the first clue at his friend, who studied it then chuckled.

"Mind, but she took a chance." Hugh went on to explain about Roana's request. "Before you ask, I do not have any ships sailing to Italy, but I might know someone who has. His company is based in Dieppe, but we have a reciprocal docking agreement. He came into port two days ago and, I believe, is due to sail to the Mediterranean in the next few days."

"Where. Is. My. Wife?" Gideon enunciated each word slowly and deliberately, his temper fraying.

"Venice, you numbskull. Do you not recall anything of your geography?" Hugh's amusement bubbled into outright laughter. "Oh, to be a fly on the wall when the two of you reunite."

The three spent the evening planning Gideon's voyage.

The following morning, Gideon accompanied Hugh to Trentams where he met Monsieur Romain, owner of the shipping company Hugh had mentioned the previous night.

It was five days until the next sailing, but Monsieur Romain — who would also captain this particular voyage — affirmed he had room on board for Gideon. His new passenger's status, and large bag of coin, added incentive.

Gideon went on to the museum. He spoke at length with the director, who proved most helpful, inspiring the earl to leave a generous donation in gratitude.

Prior to departing London, Gideon begged an interview with Lucas Withers, his boss. He explained his current circumstances, and how likely it was Lady de Beauvais' behaviour had contributed to Roana's distress.

Lucas, conversant with the marchioness'... manipulative traits, immediately assigned another — older and rather less... attractive — operative to the job, and wished Gideon, Godspeed.

During the voyage, in between doing what he could to keep boredom and a severe bout of seasickness at bay, Gideon tried to devise a plan to win Roana back. A less than happy childhood meant his wife had a tendency to conceal her true feelings, yet with him she was always open and relaxed, her trust in him, absolute. Nevertheless, he knew it did not take much for her to withdraw.

He could have kicked himself for not realising something was wrong. His excuse of being focused on his other responsibilities seemed pathetic in hindsight. He studied the letter and two riddles she left for him. *Were there more? How else would he find her in a city of thousands?*

The director of the museum had given Gideon a guide of sorts, which included a basic map of the city, as well as providing the address of the Scuola. This meant Gideon knew where Roana's colleagues would be, and he hoped they might be amenable to assisting him.

Although worried for his wife's safety, alone in a foreign country, Gideon could not help but admire her pluck. To embark on such an adventure, testament to her fortitude.

This side of Roana was as much an enigma as her puzzles, one he could not wait to unravel.

Venice

Nearly three thousand miles away, Roana was, albeit slowly, becoming more proficient in the techniques and skill necessary to blow and shape glass.

Luigi, patriarch of the Pirozzi family, who had agreed to instruct the eccentric-looking foreigner was pleased with his pupil's progress. This Signore Dumont was attentive and meticulous. Laudable traits in Luigi's opinion.

Time felt as though it was passing in the blink of an eye.

September was sliding gracefully towards October.
The sultry heat yielded as the change of season loomed.
Summer's glaring brilliance mellowed to a more subdued hue.
Venice was on the cusp of autumn.

Each evening, after dining, Roana retired to the balcony off the main bedchamber, where she watched the sunset. It was a time of contemplation, and the magical display of colour and light never failed to soothe and uplift her.

As the flaming red and orange faded to rich purple and pink, and the city sank into shadow, her thoughts inevitably winged to Gideon. *Had he decided to follow her, or was it easier to let her go?* Of course, she hoped it was the former, but she had flouted the rules by leaving without permission.

In all honesty, he had every right to have their marriage annulled for her actions, but that was a protracted and convoluted process. Maybe he would have her declared missing presumed dead. While continually questioning her own audacity, Roana trusted her intuition.

Unable to reach Gideon in any other way, even her attempts at seduction had gone unnoticed, she relied on her instincts. It required something enterprising enough to spark his interest but not infuriate him.

Roana had considered Paris, but when she overheard her colleagues discussing their trip to Venice, something clicked.

Whatever the outcome, it was too late, she could not turn back time.

In spite of the beauty everywhere she looked, of busy days, followed by quiet nights spent reading or learning Italian —

at least making a valiant attempt, Roana admitted to an underlying loneliness.

Until the last few months, Gideon and she had spent every evening together, and even if they were separately occupied, having him in the same room was enough. Moreover, there was always staff bustling about.

Here in Venice, the house was generally empty. Roana had hired a single maid. Paola, a local woman recommended by someone at the Scuola was a typical Venetian — vivacious, voluble and not afraid to speak her mind.

The two women had struck up an instant friendship and Roana enjoyed the company, but Paola had a husband and family to care for. Although Paola had offered to live in, Roana assured her new friend, she could manage on her own overnight.

For the most part, Roana welcomed the silence. To her own surprise, the hours of solitude meant she had become quite self-sufficient. If nothing else, this sojourn had taught her to stand on her own two feet, and she appreciated the morsel of independence she had gained.

None of which banished the ache in her heart when memories of Gideon strayed into her mind.

CHAPTER SIX

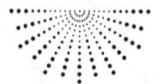

*I*t was a cool morning when *The Trident* slid into the bacino di San Marco. Gideon was riveted by the scene in front of him. Boats of all shapes and sizes bustled across a wide lagoon, bordered by some of the most beautiful buildings he had ever seen.

The captain took it upon himself to point out the different islands and landmarks. To their left the Grand Canal. Ahead — waves lapping intermittently onto the quayside — the Piazza San Marco, flanked by the Palazzo Ducale and the Bibliotheca Marciana. The gracious structures leading the eye to the extraordinary Basilica di San Marco. The Catholic cathedral of Venice.

Everywhere Gideon looked, there were buildings adorned with domes, spires, towers, and minarets, punctuated by elaborately arched colonnades, and Romanesque windows.

The Byzantine, Moorish, and Oriental influences created an enchanting vista. In the golden autumnal light, with the sun glistening on the water, the city seemed more illusion than substance.

The notion the scene would evaporate if one so much as touched it, moved Gideon to question whether he hadn't wandered into a dream.

Captain Romain informed Gideon, the gondolas — the long, narrow boats flitting about — were the main transport around the city and, although there were some pathways, they were oft underwater.

Noting the ship was nearing the dock, Gideon gathered his belongings. Thanking captain and crew, he prepared to disembark. Like Roana, he had travelled without the usual mounds of luggage and legion of staff, remarking in an aside to the captain that the lack of both was liberating, if not a trifle unnerving.

"I am sure you will be fine, Lord Brooketon. You seem to 'ave a... hmmm... 'ow does Monsieur Drummond call it... ah yes the canny head," was the French captain's considered opinion. "Your good lady 'as no doubt arranged everything just so, *n'est ce pas*? In Venice, there are always people who are looking for the decent employment. You 'ave your papers?"

Captain Romain referred to the letters of introduction should Gideon require them, and the letter of credit from his bank.

"Thank you, yes." Gideon replied, patting the breast pocket of his coat.

"Watch for pick-pockets," the captain adjured. "The wharves are rife with *les gueux*... err... I think you say the little wretches." He translated at Gideon's puzzled expression.

Gideon nodded his comprehension. "Ahhh, yes. All big cities are the same, Captain Romain," he replied, unperturbed. "Rest assured, I shall take every precaution."

They fell quiet and watched as, skilfully, the helmsman manoeuvred the vessel into its allocated berth, the surrounds of which were awash with humanity. All manner of cargo was being transferred off or on the multitude of craft rocking alongside the wooden jetties.

Once *The Trident* was moored and the gangplank lowered, Gideon made his way off the ship. His legs felt unsteady after three weeks at sea, not helped by the constant slapping of water against the dock.

He stood on the quayside trying to get his bearings.

One of the crew, a gnarly sailor, known as Hob, clumped down the gangplank behind him and offered his services.

"Cap'n sent me. I knows how to get around a bit like. Leastways I can get yer t't bank," he said by way of explanation.

Gideon accepted the offer gratefully and within the hour was being ushered into the manager's office at the aforementioned bank.

His affairs in order, Gideon arrived at his lodgings, considerately arranged by the bank manager. The luxurious furnishings exceeded anything even he was used to. Neither did this equate to comfort and, although grateful, Gideon hoped it would be temporary.

Exhausted and travel weary, he was pleased to note there was a bath, of which he made good use. All but inhaling a decent meal, he fell into bed before the evening was half over.

The next morning, Gideon located the Scuola della Carità. Opening the unassuming, aged wooden door, tucked almost out of sight, he walked into a modest atrium.

Introducing himself to the clerk seated behind the desk, Gideon asked to speak with Mr Archibald or Mr Brandisch, should either be available. He was ushered to a seat, while a student was dispatched to find the English gentlemen.

Ten minutes later, Mr Brandisch poked his head around the door to see Gideon nodding off in the peaceful vestibule. He coughed to announce his presence.

Gideon shot upright and stared at one of the men his wife had chosen to accompany. He half-expected a young, handsome bachelor, waiting to swoop in and steal Roana from him.

Mr Brandisch was quite the opposite. Elderly, a little bent with age, sporting a shock of white hair and a bushy beard, the combination of which made him look a trifle unhinged.

Gideon felt relief wash over him. Some of his concern regarding the motives of the men with whom Roana had travelled, diminished.

"Lord Brooketon." Mr Brandisch bowed. "I am Hubert Brandisch. It is a pleasure to make your acquaintance, although the circumstances are perhaps troublesome. Your arrival is more precipitous than your wife anticipated." He grinned and, unexpectedly, Gideon found himself reciprocating.

"She was not sure you would come at all. So glad, so glad. Roana will smile again." He patted Gideon's arm, in complete disregard of the younger man's status. "I believe…" he strode over to the desk and spoke to the clerk.

Gideon saw a piece of paper being passed over and allowed himself a resigned chuckle. *Really Roana, you thought it germane to drag your colleagues into your game?* He wrested his attention back to Mr Brandisch who was waving the sheet under his nose.

"There you go. Roana asked us to hand this to you, if you happened by." The nonchalant nature of the remark making it sound as though Gideon had popped around the corner not sailed half-way around Europe.

"Did she make you swear to keep the details of her accommodation secret?" Gideon quizzed.

A faint blush appeared under the white beard.

Gideon sighed. "Mr Brandisch, while I cannot demand you break a vow, I am wearied and want to find my wife. I have made haste from Brooketon Manor to London, to Venice. A not insignificant expedition as well you know."

Mr Brandisch folded his arms and studied Gideon, speculatively. Roana had not confided in either Mr Archibald or himself but when they departed England, her dejected demeanour, in contrast with her usual cheer was telling. No woman disguises herself as a man and leaves her husband — whom they knew she loved dearly — without good reason.

"Please..." Gideon's plea, quiet though it was, echoed around the atrium.

"My inclination is to deny your petition, however, the pair of you need to fix whatever is broken. I have a meeting to attend. I shall be an hour. Enough time for you to make an attempt to decipher Roana's note. If, when I return you have not solved it, I promise to give you her address."

Gideon nodded slowly. It was a fair offer. "Thank you," he said, sincerely.

Mr Brandisch bowed and, after speaking to the clerk once more, left the earl to it.

A tray with coffee and an assortment of pastries appeared by Gideon's elbow. He sipped the heady brew and ate the delicate fare absently, his concentration on what he hoped was Roana's last puzzle.

My love, you are here
My hope is renewed
My heart is still yours
If, to keep it, you choose

In a secluded square
Sits my modest abode
Its name is derived
From gondola oars

Unravel my clue
This one is the last
My friends may assist
If your patience is past

Our reunion will likely
mix ire with bliss,
but to be in your arms,
is my most fervent wish.

While my poetry is questionable,
My love remains unshakeable.
I dare to trust you feel the same
Yours, forever and always
Roana

Gideon stared at the sheet. Even her writing could set his heart racing. The flowing script reflective of her zest for life. Scrutinising the lines, he frowned. It was obvious Roana remained unsure of his affection. Her words were part teasing, part tentative.

He leant back in the chair and let his thoughts roam. His knowledge of Italian was almost non-existent, but he had studied Latin at school, and knew the former developed from the latter. It was worth a quick enquiry.

Approaching the desk, he asked the young clerk, in slow deliberate English whether there were any squares which had *remus* or *remo* as part of their name.

The lad pondered this for a while, then a stream of Italian fell from smiling lips.

Gideon lifted his hands in the easily recognisable, 'I have no idea what you are saying,' gesture, making the clerk laugh.

He motioned to the sheet of paper Gideon was holding.

Passing it across the desk, Gideon waited.

The lad dipped his quill into the small bottle of ink and scrawled *Campiello del Remer* in a spidery hand.

Gideon peered at it. "Campiello del Remer?" he quizzed.

The clerk nodded.

"Thank you. Where is that?"

Another flood of effusive Italian ensued. Gideon gave up and thanked the lad, resuming his seat at the far side of the atrium. He would wait for Mr Brandisch; it was easier.

CHAPTER SEVEN

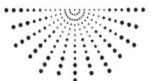

$\mathcal{W}$hile Gideon was trying to make sense of his wife's note and the desk clerk's Italian, Roana was on the little island of Murano manipulating her first major piece of blown glass.

She had achieved some success with small items, mostly beads but her tutor, the ever-patient Luigi, had encouraged her to attempt something more substantial.

She remained doubtful of her abilities but was prepared to try. Her earnest determination to conquer both glassblowing, and their language had endeared Roana to Luigi, his family and the three other apprentices. They continued to tease her unmercifully about... well... everything, but were also kind, and generous with their time.

Roana had long admitted she was no gentleman. During one lesson, the heat generated by the furnaces had caused her to become overly warm. In an attempt to cool off, and without thinking, she shoved at the floppy cap confining her hair. The inadvertent action released her thick auburn plait, which tumbled down her back, shocking all in the workshop.

Embarrassed at being caught out, she had hastened to

explain the reason for her disguise in halting Italian. It transpired, trousers and shirts were safer clothing anyway because women's gowns were prone to catching fire. Thus, Roana continued as she had begun and had worn a gown only occasionally since her arrival in Venice.

Long wooden benches sported tubs of ready-mixed ingredients. The process of glassblowing was not uncomplicated and involved two furnaces. The first was used to melt a material resembling fine sand with something Luigi called flux to form a *fritta*, which was then added to waste glass chips and melted in the second fire.

At this stage, other elements were added to produce the various colours, all of which had Italian names. Roana could never remember one from the other, so chose at random, resulting in what could only be described as unique hues and odd blotches.

Since she was not planning to sell any of the pieces she made, Roana didn't care, relieved she had managed to forge something even vaguely recognisable.

By the end of the afternoon, with a little assistance from Elio, Luigi's son, who took over when Roana could not blow any more, she had a bowl. It was a little wavy around the rim and wobbled a bit when she placed it on a flat surface, but it was definitely a bowl.

"*Grazie, grazie mille.*" She clapped her grubby hands gleefully, unaware her face was sooty from the wood smoke and her attire while protected by a heavy apron, was not much better. She glanced outside and noticed the setting sun.

"*Devo andare,*" Roana said, washing her hands in the sink. Running damp fingers through her hair, she twisted it up and tucked it under her cap, pulling the brim low over her forehead.

Luigi chuckled. "Go then, Elio will take you. Will you come tomorrow?"

"All being well, yes please... err... *dopo mezzogiorno?*" Hoping she was saying after midday.

"After the noon?" Luigi arched a quizzical brow.

Roana grinned in relief and nodded. *"Si."*

Patting her hands dry on her trousers, she smiled gratefully at Elio who had brought her cloak. It was hot in the workshop, but the nights had turned cold and the breeze off the sea was apt to be frigid when the day waned.

Soon they were skimming over water, which reminded Roana of the glass she had been working with — smooth and sensuous. The lagoon glowed in the setting sun as though fires smouldered beneath the surface. The breeze had dropped, and the gentle ripples shimmered in radiant iridescence.

Roana would never tire of the ride back to Cannaregio.

Cloaked by the gloaming, the floating city settled down for the evening. The only sounds as Elio rowed — the cry of the seagulls or the hail of another gondolier.

The splendour of Venice was almost indescribable, and Roana knew she was fortunate indeed to witness it every day.

Elio moored the gondola beside the little square where Roana lived. After helping her out, he was back in the boat and waving a goodnight. She could hear him whistling as he navigated the narrow waterway back onto the Grand Canal; the tune reverberating off the buildings.

She stood for a moment and stretched, her back aching a little from bending over the workbench. She lifted the bowl and paused, letting the last rays of the sun reflect through it, then shivered. Too chilly to loiter.

Removing her hat, Roana shook her head. Released from its confines, the heavy plait uncoiled like a rope. She blew a thankful sigh that her hair was no longer restricted under the snug cap.

Walking across the square, she did not see a tall figure peel out of the shadows, nor did she hear him fall into step behind her. His feet, silent on the flagstones. She was completely unaware of another presence until, as she lifted the latch on the heavy wooden door, a man spoke behind her ear.

"You dare to wander the streets alone." A hint of suppressed anger in the deep voice.

Roana shrieked with fright and, flinging her arms out presumably to ward off her unseen attacker, spun around so rapidly she lost her footing. Colliding heavily with the door, which swung open, Roana landed with a bump on the unforgiving tiles, air whooshing out of her lungs.

Winded and slightly stunned, she raised her head, trying to think of how to deal with an intruder, when she recognised the man looming over her in the half-light.

Her husband!

"G-Gideon?" Her mouth fell open in shock and she scrambled to her feet. The glass bowl still clutched in her hand.

"You were expecting someone else?" He made no move to assist her.

Unnerved and heart hammering, Roana gaped at her tall, handsome husband in disbelief. She questioned, briefly, whether this was her imagination or a dream, while banking down the desire to hurl herself at him, beat on his chest with her fists, burst into tears, then hold on and never let go.

He had come but was it to rebuke or... she couldn't finish that thought; not ready to hear the answer. At the sound of a throat clearing, she realised he was awaiting her response.

"I was not expecting anyone, hence my... errr... immoderate reaction."

"Small mercies, I suppose."

Roana searched Gideon's face. His expression gave nothing away. Her stomach knotted and she felt a sensation, something akin to grief trickle down her spine.

Her shoulders drooped and she closed her eyes. *What did she expect?* She had left. Walked away with what could be construed as careless indifference as to how her disappearance might affect her husband.

Despite a tiny corner of her heart clinging to the hope he would follow, Roana had resigned herself to the improbability. Suddenly, he was here, right in front of her, but it was nearly three months since last they saw each other. He was like a stranger.

Straightening her shoulders, she opened her eyes and braved his gaze. "W-would you like to c-come in?" she stammered her invitation.

"Thank you." Gideon stepped into the dim entrance hall. He closed the door, dropped the latch and turned the great iron key.

Roana led the way upstairs to the second floor where she spent most of her time.

On the dining table, where she placed the little bowl, stood two platters of food covered with a piece of cloth. Roana sent a silent prayer of thanks to Paola for preparing this light meal. Closing the shutters against the brisk air, she lit a handful of candelabra. The soft glimmer gave the room a pleasing ambience.

There was nothing more she could do, to delay the inevitable.

With a resigned huff, Roana faced her husband.

CHAPTER EIGHT

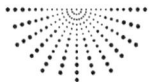

*G*ideon had found the small square an hour or so before Roana returned. Rapping on the door, he was surprised when a woman who was not his wife opened it.

He introduced himself and, after Paola responded in kind, showed her one of the letters he carried to affirm his identity should it prove necessary.

Paola remained unwilling to permit him entry. She knew nothing of Roana's life in England and the protective Italian woman was not about to let just anyone inside her mistress' home, earl or not.

Although piqued, Gideon found he respected her loyalty and assured her, he would wait outside for his wife. Paola was torn, he looked so weary, but her allegiance was to Roana not this stranger. She offered him a hot drink and some food, but that was all, trusting her mistress would understand her decision.

. . .

Twilight had fallen when Gideon heard voices on the breeze. A gondola cruised to a halt at the edge of the square. The gondolier leapt onto the path to assist a second occupant out of the boat.

Gideon watched their interaction abstractedly, more to pass the time than for any other reason. The passenger thanked the boatman and stood for a moment, tilting back his head and rolling his shoulders as though they were stiff.

Gideon saw him lift an object. The blood red of the dying sun shone right through it. Not close enough to make out what it was, to Gideon it looked quite fragile.

The man removed his cap and there was the sound of a deep sigh. Gideon blinked, certain his eyes deceived him. A waist-length plait tumbled down the man's back and he shook his head as though relishing its liberty.

Gideon swallowed on a startled gasp.

Something about the gesture resonated with him.

It was Roana.

Myriad emotions flooded through Gideon.

Relief at finding Roana safe and unharmed.

Grudging admiration that she possessed the mettle to undertake so perilous a journey in the first place.

Joy that after three months apart, his wife was within arm's reach of him.

All, *God forgive him*, tinged with ire at her imprudence, and the despair she had put him through. Conveniently forgetting it was he who instigated the fiasco.

The devil inside goaded Gideon to creep up behind Roana. As she lifted the latch, he spoke next to her ear, totally unprepared for her scream and ungainly stumble.

To his everlasting shame, he did not offer to help her up.

Instead, he stood with arms folded, by which time it was too late. Roana was on her feet, spluttering his name.

He saw her bite her lip to stop it trembling, her face ashen in the gloom. That he had scared his wife left Gideon feeling like an unmitigated cad, stubbornly refusing to acknowledge the minuscule sense of satisfaction her response engendered.

He heard himself reply and willed his brain to stop his lips from uttering oblique accusations. Never once had Roana given him reason to suspect she was anything other than faithful. She believed *he* was the one having the affair.

His reactions were triggered by his own insecurities, exacerbated when his wife did *not* fling herself into his arms, as he expected.

In truth, he was terrified she would refuse to return home with him.

That his incautious behaviour with Constance de Beauvais had killed Roana's love.

Not that he was disposed to acknowledge the possibility… yet.

Roana — to Gideon's growing unease — somewhat unenthusiastically, invited him in. She led him up two flights of stairs to a charmingly appointed room. While she pottered about lighting candles, Gideon studied his surroundings. Unsure what to expect, his own lodgings bordering on obscenely opulent, he was pleasantly surprised at the simplicity of the domain.

The floor was tiled. The creamy colour alleviated here and there by a random scattering of terracotta, blue, and yellow. The furniture, although minimal and obviously of good quality looked to have been chosen for comfort.

A marble topped, wrought-iron dining table — on which Roana had placed the wobbly glass bowl — stood against one wall. Two straight-backed chairs with cushioned seats were tucked underneath, neatly.

A chaise and two over-stuffed chairs circled a sizeable fireplace. Remnants of gnarly logs burned low in the grate, and he welcomed the residual heat thrown out. At one side of the hearth — a basket full of chopped wood; at the other — a squat, rustic-style table, laden with books.

Gideon felt a smile tug at his lips. Books were like food to Roana, and she tended to have several on the go at once. How she worked out which story was which never ceased to confound him.

The room, despite its length was relatively narrow and might have felt confined save for the high ceiling, which gave the impression of a much larger space. At either end, two arched windows, currently shuttered, flanked a set of French doors. Positioned in front of the doors closest to him, a sofa and a footstool.

On a low table beside the sofa — piled precariously — more books, and what looked like a journal, complete with ink pot and quill. Gideon knew Roana to be an avid diarist and shuddered to think of how he was portrayed in it, latterly.

Roana hovered by the dining table, her posture, rigid.

Gideon ran his eyes over his wife, taking in her masculine attire, registering how well it suited her. Under a waistcoat of silver and green brocade, she wore a grubby-looking shirt. With surprise, Gideon recognised it to be one of his. It was coming untucked from a pair of grey breeches which, being at the bare minimum a size too big, Roana had rolled up at the ankles.

Flaunting her ankles, for shame! Oh, but they were so shapely. He itched to stroke them.

Her footwear resembled the rope-soled shoes worn by gondoliers and dockhands. *Damned, if they didn't look comfort-*

able. Her face was smudged with what Gideon surmised might well be soot, prompting him to question what the dickens his wife had been up to when not at the Scuola.

Rich auburn hair hung over one shoulder, glossy tendrils escaping from the thick plait. Restless fingers worried the hem of her shirt, the soft cotton swiftly becoming more bedraggled. This, together with the pulse he could see fluttering in her neck and her pallor, revealed her discomposure.

"Roana..." he hesitated then went on, "...why?"

She gaped at him. *He had to ask? He had come all this way, followed her clues...* her heart swelled a little — he had followed her clues — *no, she was still angry with him... and he still didn't know why?*

"Y-you do n-not know?" she stuttered, incredulously.

He spread his hands. "Only what you wrote in your letter."

"Is that not enough?" Roana demanded, her temper — as fiery as her hair — threatening to spill over.

"You think being the brunt of malicious gossip, to see you hold another in your arms, of being laughed at *to my face* because I cannot keep my husband *satisfied*," she sneered the word, "is not enough? To be ignored in our own home by the man I believed loved me above all others, or the searing humiliation when my attempt to seduce him, is met by a blank stare, is not **enough**?

"What more do you want, Gideon? I tried *everything* to get you to talk to me. To tell me what I had done to precipitate such indifference. Have you *any* idea how many nights I cried myself to sleep or walked the halls because slumber eluded me? No, of course you haven't. **You were not there**.

"Even when we were together you were distant, preoccupied. I accept my decision to come here, to run away was inconsiderate, drastic even. Believe me, I did not take it lightly. It was my last resort."

She sucked in a breath and flipped her hand. "You read my letters. You solved my puzzles. *Something* motivated you to follow me, to find me, yet you could not be bothered to help me up after causing me to fall. How can you *possibly* say you do not know what provoked me to act thus?"

Dumbfounded by Roana's outrage, while mesmerised by her glittering green eyes and vivid countenance, Gideon felt panic coil through him. *Had he already lost her?*

He hastened to clarify, "Roana, please, forgive me. I was not questioning *why* you fled, more why so far away? Why Venice? Why not Wales or Scotland? The dangers of you travelling alone..." he faltered. The nightmare of his wife being drowned at sea, or attacked by pirates or bandits or basically anyone, rearing up in his mind.

The deep timbre of Gideon's voice enveloped Roana.

She heard the dread he was unable to mask.

Abruptly, the whys and wherefores paled in consequence. They needed to be addressed. She wanted an explanation for his recent behaviour, to understand what provoked it, and whether he had indulged in a liaison with *that* woman.

Yes, a discussion was imperative but, right at that moment, Roana cared for naught save her husband was *here*, in Venice, *with her.*

"Gideon..." she held his gaze. Her eyes wary. "Why did you come?"

"Because I love you."

CHAPTER NINE

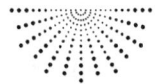

*S*ilence fell between them like a pall.

The pop and hiss of the fire was the only sound to break the strained quiet.

Roana took a step towards her husband, then hesitated.

His declaration was all well and good but, if he loved her, why had he behaved so callously?

"Roana, please, allow me to explain."

She studied Gideon, as dispassionately as possible. No easy feat because she loved him too... more than ever, *damn the man*.

Tall — he was head and shoulders taller than she, and Roana was not short — with hair, so dark brown it was almost black. Brown eyes, the colour of freshly brewed coffee — velvety, fathomless, set in a face which, although rather angular was softened by the beard hugging his jaw. A beard grown since last she saw him. Usually, he was clean shaven.

Roana had to acknowledge, the faintly dangerous air it gave her husband, suited him, deliberately quelling the thrill of excitement *that* idea elicited.

Tan breeches encased Gideon's strapping legs. A white shirt under a dull-bronze paisley-patterned waistcoat hid his muscular torso. His dark cream cravat was askew, its rakish angle pulling the hint of a smile to her lips.

The ensemble was completed by a fine wool jacket in burnt umber, which happened to be a favourite of Roana's. Awkwardness aside, she was inordinately pleased he had selected this coat to wear for their reunion.

Standing with his feet apart, hands loosely clasped behind him, Gideon exuded power and charisma.

Roana, as she so often did, pondered what it was about her which had attracted him.

She nodded and, not quite trusting herself to speak, opened one palm, tacitly inviting him to continue.

Gideon caught the quirk of Roana's lips. The gesture slowed the ice snaking down his spine. Mentally steeling himself, he started at the beginning, with the death of Simon de Beauvais, ending with his arrival here, tonight.

It took some time because he was determined to tell her everything; surmising this might be the one chance to win back his wife.

Roana listened carefully, while he clarified his relationship, or lack thereof, with Lady de Beauvais. The candour in his voice was not feigned, convincing her as little else would.

To be scrupulously fair, Gideon, although a shrewd investigator — clever when it came to interpreting documents or extracting information — was somewhat naive when it came to women and their wiles.

He would never suspect a woman was deliberately trying to worm her way into his affections. Moreover, had he wanted to bed the countess, he would have no reason to follow her, Roana, to Venice. Once his wife was out of sight and out of mind, he could act without hindrance.

As he concluded, Gideon watched Roana absorb his words. Her expressive face more eloquent than she realised.

"On my oath, I never intended to hurt you or make you believe I no longer loved you. Ro, you are the other half of me. Without you, my life has no meaning."

"Gideon, I know you believe what you say, but the sorrow I suffered prior to my departure for Venice, lingers. Your death would have been less traumatic. I actually questioned whether maybe *I* had died and become a ghost because, to you, I did not exist.

"After all we had been to each other. How was that even possible? Was I an inadequate wife in some way? Was it, mayhap, because I have yet to bear you a child?" Aware tears threatened, Roana pressed her lips together, firmly. She would *not* give in to weeping — she had no patience for feminine nonsense.

"What happens if I return to London with you and a similar situation arises, which assuredly it will. My love, I respect your dedication to your job with Lucas, and your parliamentary responsibilities. I do not wish, nor do I expect you to give them up, but when your loyalty to either comes at the expense of your commitment to me, to our marriage, I cannot see the point. Once was bad enough..."

Roana was trembling. Giving her husband an ultimatum, however gently couched, would probably not end well.

Gideon strained to hear Roana's words, stunned she thought him so shallow as to use their lack of children as an excuse to stray. Her voice dwindled as she came to the end of her little speech.

He spotted the tears misting her eyes and the occasional tremor running through her willowy frame, disgusted with himself for being the one to inflict such desolation.

Dammit, he was losing her all over again.

Could a heart actually splinter?

His whole world began to crash down around him.

At a loss, Gideon was about to concede defeat, temporarily, when out of the blue it came to him.

Roana's greatest fear was *not* other women, or gossip. Yes, such things were... inconvenient, but not unusual in their rarefied world and under normal circumstances, she had the confidence to rise above the naysayers.

It was being ignored.

Of believing herself so insignificant in his life, he would turn to another.

He closed his eyes. *How in the hell had he let it go so badly wrong?* In truth, it was quite simple. His love for Roana transcended everything... his job, his family, his friends, his status... everything.

Could he rectify his mistake?

Two words gave him hope — she had called him 'my love'.

Gideon took a gamble.

Stepping forward he reached out and untangled her

fingers from her shirt. His large hand engulfed her much smaller one and he drew her against him.

Roana stared, hypnotised by his fingers, which she swore possessed magical powers. They could reduce her to a quivering heap with the slightest touch. The thought of which increased her heart rate, as she became aware his thumb was drawing slow circles on her palm.

"G-Gideon," she croaked, vexed that she sounded so... needy.

"Roana..."

The murmur of her name from his lips was irresistible and she could feel her resolve weakening. She forced herself to concentrate as he spoke.

"I unravelled your clues. I followed you halfway around the world. I love you."

She felt his lips brush her forehead.

"You have my word I will never, ever treat you as an after-thought, or relegate you to second place. I have loved you since first we met and, forgetting my pledge to cherish you, confess I have taken your love for granted." He kissed the sensitive spot behind her ear.

She heard a moan... *good gracious that was **her**... brazen hussy.*

"It was never my intent to cause you such pain or distress that to flee was your only recourse."

His mouth grazed her neck to the hollow at the base of her throat. Incapable of controlling her reactions, Roana's head fell back, exposing her satiny skin, an unspoken invitation. He took full advantage, burning a trail of kisses to the rise of her breasts.

. . .

"Forgive me, my love." Gideon pulled the shirt out of her breeches, fingers skimming over her warm skin. He heard her sigh. "Forgive me." His hand slid around her waist, his fingers splaying over her back. "Please, Roana, love of my life, heart of my heart, please forgive me."

He captured her mouth with his, his tongue seeking hers. The tips touched and the smouldering embers flared into life. Roana succumbed... being loved was far more rewarding than being righteously indignant.

Their kiss deepened and passion swirled, but Gideon held it at bay, taking his time, letting the ardour build. This was not something to be rushed, they had been apart too long.

Night shrouded the city. A harvest moon guarded by millions of twinkling stars blanketed Venice in an ethereal glow. Temperatures plummeted as biting winds whipped over the water, causing boats to rock on their moorings, and any unlucky souls who happened to be abroad to complain, while huddling into heavy coats.

None of this was noticed by Gideon and Roana, who — not in the slightest bit cold — lost all sense of time and place as they rediscovered their love for each other.

CHAPTER TEN

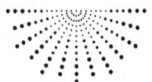

*D*uring the ensuing days, Gideon and Roana hardly left the house. Roana sent an apology to Luigi explaining why she was unable to attend his workshop, while Gideon arranged to have his luggage transferred to his wife's lodgings.

From time to time, they ventured out for a stroll, or a ride along the canals. While Roana showed Gideon around this city with which she was so enamoured, they began to talk.

Prior to this recent... predicament, the couple had enjoyed open and honest communication. From the moment they met, they had revelled in spirited debate as much as quiet conversation. Matters dear to their hearts were discussed with enthusiasm not ignored, and they never had any problem chatting about things considered personal, private, and intimate.

It was one of their greatest strengths. One sorely lacking of late.

To this facet of their relationship, especially Roana's letter and the reason they ended up in Venice, the couple directed all their attention...

...well not quite *all*!

*

Autumn, known as the most unpredictable season weather-wise, held Venice in its grip. By and large, the city basked in days of uninterrupted sunshine, but there were periods when everything was enveloped in fog. It crept in like tendrils of ivy, clinging to everything, muffling sound and light — giving the city an unearthly aspect.

Just when the greyness seemed unending, the breeze strengthened, driving the wraithlike mist out of the canals and squares until, at last, it evaporated, and it seemed as though Venice was reborn in the sunlight.

The capricious nature of the season could be frustrating, not to mention a harbinger of winter, and prompted many of the local elite to travel south to warmer climes.

To Roana and Gideon, made from sterner stuff and familiar with the vagaries of English weather, it merely added to the magic that was Venice. An experience not to be missed.

Intermittently, rain and wind lashed the city bringing with it warnings of *acqua alta*. Paola explained this *acqua alta*, or high water, occurred in autumn and spring, and often caused widespread flooding.

"It is like too much tide," she elaborated one morning, in her limited English, while serving breakfast. "If it 'appens, we get wet, then it goes. *Normale.*" She shrugged.

It was of no importance to her. An annual phenomenon the Venetians lived with. Yes, it was inconvenient, but they were used to it. Foreigners tended to panic, believing the city was sinking... *tsk, how ridiculous!*

These two seemed quite sensible and took most things in

their stride, confirmed seconds later when Roana asked whether she would still be able to take a boat to Murano.

"Of course! Water is water. High or low, life continues." Paola gave another shrug, the casual gesture making Roana grin. "Today is sunny, no problem."

"*Grazie*, Paola." she said, and turned to Gideon. "Would you like to see what I've been doing?"

"Nothing would give me greater pleasure." He smiled at her eager face.

Presently, they were on their way to the little island. Gideon was welcomed by Luigi and his family and, after watching a demonstration, pronounced himself astonished by their expertise. He was persuaded to try his hand at glassblowing and made a creditable effort.

Roana gave her husband a tour of Murano, explaining why so few glassblowers retained their workshops. By the end of the day, following a lengthy discussion with Luigi and Elio, a plan began to brew in Gideon's mind. As they were ferried to Cannaregio, he broached the subject with Roana.

"It seems for want of a little funding, these artisans will struggle to continue. Their livelihoods, and an ancient skill, at risk of being lost."

Roana peered at Gideon in the waning light. "I think it highly likely. I do not know how they have survived to date. Napoleon all but crushed the industry into non-existence. 'Tis only by the grace of God and the patronage of a handful of the Venetian aristocracy, any continue to function. Why?"

"I am considering investing in Luigi's workshop. I confess I am fascinated by the ability to fabricate pieces of extraordinary beauty from something as mundane as sand. The demise of their talent would be a travesty.

"Moreover, it would necessitate us coming every eighteen months or so, to check on the business. Something I deem most beneficial. To visit Italy, let alone this incredible city, never entered my head. Although I sincerely regret the reason you fled here, I am profoundly glad you did. Do you think Luigi might be amenable to my proposal?"

Roana's beaming smile was answer enough, but she snuggled close and brushed her lips to his cheek.

"I think that is the most splendid idea you have ever had."

Gideon slipped an arm around her shoulders and drew her against him, pressing a kiss to her forehead.

"No, my darling. My most splendid idea was asking you to marry me."

Which, of course elicited another kiss.

"I am eternally grateful I did not ruin what we share, and get to spend the rest of my life unravelling you, one way or another."

He heard a soft chuckle.

"Why, Lord Brooketon, are you trying to seduce me?" Roana pretended to fan herself.

"Every chance I get, Lady Brooketon." His voice a low growl.

"What a shame we are still on the water," Roana teased.

"Not for much longer."

The Rio Terà Barba Frutariol came into view. Seconds later, Elio docked the gondola at the Campiello del Remer. The couple were out and across the tiny square calling their hurried thanks and a goodbye to Elio, who shook his head and grinned in the gloom.

After a meal eaten yet barely tasted, Gideon and Roana were standing on the balcony of their bedchamber watching the ever-changing display of celestial light.

Gideon, who found he preferred his wife in men's clothing — it made undressing her even more satisfying — lifted her hair to sprinkle kisses along her neck.

"You and Venice are alike in so many ways," he murmured. Turning Roana to face him, he unbuttoned her waistcoat, sliding it off her shoulders, the material hissing when it crumpled onto the tiles.

Roana tilted her head in silent question, her eyes darkening, and her heart drumming.

Gideon trailed a teasing finger down the open neck of her shirt, to pause just above the shadowy dip between her breasts. "She is known as *La Serenissima*, the Serene One because she appears tranquil and unperturbed, successfully avoiding the trials faced by other cities. You are also thus, your demeanour composed even under the most arduous circumstances."

"A generous simile, but I am rarely serene, nor do I avoid trials, as our being here attests," she retorted in ironic amusement, then her breath caught when, in one swift movement, her shirt joined the waistcoat. Roana shivered in the frosty air.

Gideon chuckled. "Fair point, my love, and perhaps we ought to take this inside."

Grasping Roana's hand, he led her into the warmth of their bedchamber. The fire crackling in the grate, the only light. Shadows leapt wildly over the walls.

Gideon proceeded to divest his wife of the remainder of her clothes. The beat of his heart tripling when Roana returned the favour — with tortuous slowness.

He lowered her onto their bed.

"To uncover the mystery that is *you*, is like discovering

this city. A riddle to be solved. A treasure revealed. Each one, priceless." he began to weave his sorcery, "I love that you are my puzzle, my conundrum, my Roana."

"Gideon?" Roana, certain she was liquifying like molten glass under his masterful touch, moaned her plea.

"Yes, my love."

"Unravel me!"

With intoxicating fervency, Gideon obliged!

EPILOGUE

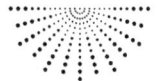

VENICE ~ APRIL 1829

*R*oana sighed with pleasure when the city, floating on a sparkling azure sea, appeared as though by magic. A veil drawn aside to reveal a hidden jewel.

The voyage, although uneventful, had been monotonous and, after nearly a month of constant rocking, Roana was anxious to stand on solid ground.

Leaning on the rail of *The Eurybia*, she admired the tranquil scene. A peace broken only by the rhythmic flap of the sails billowing overhead, the swish of the waves rippling along the hull, and the keening of the gulls.

Her solitary reverie was interrupted when a large hand came to rest on her waist.

"Good morning, my love. I thought I might find you here."

A light kiss landed on her hair.

Roana turned around to meet the amused gaze of her husband.

"You know how I relish the early mornings. The hint of mist hovering over the water. The sharp tang in the air. The grey pearlescence of the dawn becoming dazzling blue as the sun rises. 'Tis perfection. Better still..." she waved her hand in the direction they were headed.

"Ahhh... *La Serenissima*," Gideon tucked his wife against him, and they watched the land mass increase as the ship ate up the last few miles. "I was beginning the wonder whether she had drifted away, to vanish forever."

"She would not dare," Roana replied, with a grin. "She knows how we love her. Oh, Gideon, a year, a whole year. Think of the places we might visit." She clapped her hands, all but crowing with glee. "It is a boon indeed to be afforded an extended expedition, and I have been looking forward to it for an age."

⁂

In the decade since the Brooketons' first visit to Venice, they had returned as often as their responsibilities permitted. Prior to their departure for England, all those years ago, Gideon had tracked down the owner of Roana's lodgings and offered him an exorbitant amount to purchase it.

Signore Caselli all but shook Gideon's hand off. Ecstatic to divest himself of the old building at so inflated a price. *Foreigners, tsk, they were molto impazzito... crazy.* Not that he was complaining or prepared to negotiate more reasonable terms. *This Lord Brooketon wanted to pay, he, Signore Caselli, would not deny him that pleasure.*

Gideon knew he had overpaid, but the cost mattered little. Despite their brevity of residence, the tall, narrow, house had become more than a temporary dwelling. To a couple rekindling a love almost lost, it had become a haven, then a home.

Without losing the rustic ambience, which was what appealed to Roana in the first place, they had inspected each level thoroughly, and refurbished where necessary. On subsequent trips, a few favourite comforts from the Manor were added, but that was all. Essentially, it remained the same simple abode.

Their respective families declared the couple addled for choosing to undertake what was considered a perilous journey with such frequency. They should have saved their collective breath. All attempts to dissuade, had the opposite effect.

To make Venice — for want of a better description — their sanctuary; a place to unwind and relax, a place of renewal and revival was a decision neither Roana nor Gideon regretted.

Unexpected circumstances had delayed this visit. Roana, who was starting to question whether their return might be wishful thinking, yearned to be back in the city which never failed to enchant.

❧

Captain Richards, who had been chatting to his helmsman, came to join the earl and countess.

"Good morning, my friends. At this rate, we'll be docked by midday." He gave them a cheery smile.

"Thank you, Captain. I confess, my sea legs are not too steady this journey." Roana replied, with a wry grimace.

"'Tis because you are out of practice." The burly captain chuckled. "By the time you have spent a year skimming around the canals on gondolas, you will be nicely prepared for the journey home."

"You make us sound like a pair of geese about to be stuffed," Gideon interjected.

His repost elicited a burst of laughter, and the trio fell

into animated conversation about their respective plans. Aware time was passing, Roana left the men to it, remarking she needed to check on their entourage.

As a rule, Roana and Gideon travelled with the bare minimum of luggage and no staff.

This time was slightly different.

⁂

Shortly after their previous sojourn to Venice, Roana discovered she was increasing. Given that in their fifteen years of marriage, the only time husband and wife had not shared a bed was when the latter ran away, Roana had long resigned herself to the fact, she was unable to bear a child.

Not every marriage was blessed with children, and the Brooketons' lack thereof, had meant they were free to do as they pleased.

She pretended not to hear the oft-voiced consternation of his family, while steadfastly dismissing her own desire to provide Gideon with an heir. Moreover, in her heart of hearts, Roana wasn't certain she possessed the instincts to be a mother anyway.

To be informed — at thirty-three years old — she was expecting a baby, came as a tremendous shock. Roana walked around in a daze for a week.

Gideon was equally stunned, then terrified. Childbirth was not without risk when the mother was young and, although healthy, Roana was considered well beyond child-bearing age. Her doctor deemed it a miracle she had conceived at all.

The dread he might lose his wife... again, and this time

irrevocably… turned Gideon into the proverbial mother hen. He cosseted Roana within an inch of her life.

Initially, she basked under his earnest vigilance but, eventually, she balked and, as kindly as possible, called a halt.

"My love, while I delight in your concern for my well-being, I am not made of glass. I will not shatter if I take a constitutional, or write letters, or spend an hour at the museum. I promise to take every care, but I cannot move without you panicking.

"If you continue to prevent me from going about my days, I shall be left with no alternative but to determine when the next ship to Venice will depart," Roana had warned, in the sweetest tones she could muster.

"Forgive me. I had no mind to clip your wings, 'tis only…" he had apologised. Unwilling to articulate his fear, he had tried to divert her with a lingering kiss.

"I know what bothers you, Gideon. I love you for it, but I am pregnant, not infirm. Yes, I know the hazards, and am careful not to overdo it. Your support, and the attention you lavish on me makes me feel like a queen, but perhaps you might moderate it… just a little." She had entreated, returning his kiss with interest, assuaging his anxiety the best way she knew how.

It worked… more or less.

There was another shock to come. During a doctor's appointment a few weeks prior to the birth, Roana was flabbergasted to learn she was carrying twins. The tables were turned. Now, *she* was the one panicking, while Gideon became composure personified.

He countered her contention — that this was a disaster of epic proportions, that she was not capable of looking after *one* infant never mind two, that she was too old to be a mother, the list went on — with calm reason.

When that failed to mollify, Gideon had observed, blandly, "Sweetheart, exactly what am I supposed to do? If you are so concerned, we will give one away."

As anticipated, his remark provoked the desired effect.

"Give up my baby, *our* baby? Gideon Dumont how dare you suggest such a thing?" Roana had squeaked, affronted at the mere notion.

"In that case, do stop fretting. This is not a disaster, and we *will* muddle through. I think you might be surprised at how capable we are."

The birth, while arduous and protracted was forgotten the instant Roana looked upon the faces of her newborns. Her exhaustion fled when she held them. The wonder that she was party to creating such perfection — overwhelming.

Two pairs of bleary blue eyes gazed up at her. Her son and her daughter. Roana blinked back a rush of tears, a wave of love cascading over her. Its strength — almost incomprehensible.

For once in her life, she was speechless.

"My darling, you are amazing." Gideon brushed damp strands of hair off Roana's flushed face. "I thought my heart was full, but it seems there was a little extra room." He pressed a tender kiss to his wife's temple.

Roana grasped his hand, her eyes glazing over as fatigue staked its claim. "I think I might be a trifle unravelled," she muttered, to the confusion of all save one in the room. "Are we prepared for this riddle?

"I think you might be right," Gideon murmured, as the midwife lifted the drowsy infants out of Roana's arms to tuck them in the crib.

"Sleep, my love. Time enough to puzzle this out when you are rested. I suspect it is one which will take us a lifetime to solve."

The twins' arrival wrought havoc on the lives of their parents, who embraced the chaos. Typically, Gideon and Roana did not hire an army of nursemaids, preferring to nurture their children themselves.

Yes, they made mistakes; that was to be expected, and far outweighed by the rewards. The adjustment was slow, but they rose to the challenge with characteristic equanimity.

Unwilling to encumber their offspring with any of the archaic, and to Roana's mind, dreary, names, the couple eschewed the traditions employed by both families. Even the reconciliation, of sorts, effected by the twin's birth was not enough to sway the new parents.

Roana's passion for history was reflected in the names Gideon and she selected. Camilla — Virgil's legendary maiden warrior, and Felix — happy and fortunate. Choices which were proving apt, especially Camilla who was an intrepid soul... much like her Mama.

For almost three years, Roana set aside her hankering for Venice, focused on raising the twins.

When 1829 dawned, the family were snowbound at Brooketon Manor. The weeks of enforced confinement, triggered Roana's wanderlust, inspiring her to raise with Gideon, the possibility of resuming their regular trips to Italy.

Her husband, similarly desirous, concurred with alacrity, and they began to plan.

. . .

The Season was not even half over when they embarked on *The Eurybia*. The same ship on which Roana had travelled ten years ago. An auspicious sign, in her considered opinion.

Now they had arrived. Venice was within their sights.

❧

By day's end the four Dumonts, along with their skeleton staff were safely ensconced in the charming abode in Campiello del Remer.

The ever-faithful Paola, apprised of their impending arrival by letter, had aired the house, prepared a meal, and was on the doorstep to greet them.

The two families had become good friends over the years, with Roana and Gideon being declared honorary aunt and uncle to Paola's children — who were thrilled to meet the twins.

❧

Once the two rambunctious toddlers were in bed, under the watchful eye of their nurserymaid. Roana and Gideon retired to their suite.

They stood on the balcony and watched the sun sink below the rooftops. Ribbons of purple and orange fire spiralled out into a darkening sky. The familiar and flamboyant brilliance offering the perfect backdrop to their first night in Venice.

"I cannot quite believe we are here," Roana murmured leaning into Gideon, whose arms came around her.

He rested his chin on her head. "I confess, I am inclined to question whether we are dreaming."

"If so, 'tis a good dream. Gideon, we have been away too long. Never again. Promise me."

"As I have breath in me, I promise."

"We have come so far, and not just in miles. Do you remember the evening you found me here?

"How could I forget? That was the night *I* almost came unravelled."

Roana heard the mirth in her husband's voice.

"Your discomfiture was well deserved," she retorted, pertly. "Mind, I'm endlessly glad my ploy worked," she added, ingenuously. "I feared it would backfire."

Gideon turned her to face him and brushed his lips to hers. "It was well played, my darling, but I am pleased your puzzles of late are less... shall we say... dramatic." He chuckled.

"You think having twins is *less* dramatic? They make running away seem like a picnic in Hyde Park."

They bantered back and forth, until the cool evening air prompted Gideon to draw his wife inside.

"But the stars..." Roana lamented.

"...will be there tomorrow. I can think of better things to do right now."

"You can?" She twinkled at him, mischief in her eyes.

He nodded.

"Such as?"

"This." Gideon cupped her face, his mouth seeking hers in a searing kiss.

Roana looped her arms around his neck, feeling Gideon's hands begin to weave their spell. Her body hummed. Her heart thudded.

The simmering ardour, as intense now as the day they wed almost twenty years ago, blazed into life. Its incandescence matching the radiance of the sunset.

Clothes flew in all directions.

"Gideon…" his name slipped on a sigh.

"Roana…" he echoed her tone.

"I do believe I am need of unravelling. Do you know anyone who might be g-gifted with the r-requisite s-skill?" She stuttered as his fingers reached their goal.

"I know of only one who has honed so special a talent," he growled, his lips teasing over skin prickling in anticipation.

"Do I know him?" she quipped, breathlessly.

Gideon's reply was to demonstrate his expertise.

Darkness cloaked the city.

The only illumination, a silvery moon, which transformed the humble canals into a gossamer cobweb.

All fell quiet.

While Venice slept, Gideon unravelled his wife with exquisite and consummate finesse…

…Roana surrendered.

EXCERPT FROM FATE IS CURIOUS

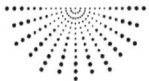

END OF SEPTEMBER ~ 1825

*C*harlotte Hastings, Countess of Sherbrooke, stood on one of the balconies of a graceful four-storey house on the *rue d'Anjou*, just off the *rue du Faubourg Saint Honoré* in Paris. She had been standing there for what seemed an age.

When she walked out onto the ornate parapet, the sun had yet to begin its descent to the horizon. Now, it had set, and the dazzling blue of the sky had morphed through a glorious fiery red to a pinkish-grey — the muted hue mirroring her sombre mood.

For, to Charlotte, it was as though everything had stopped. Life would never be the same again.

Oliver, her heart, her soul, her forever — had gone. Just like that, in what felt like the blink of an eye, he was no more. She refused to believe it. One minute he was holding her hand, telling her he loved her, then it was though someone had snuffed out the last candle in the world.

The light faded from his eyes, and his hand slipped out of hers to lie, limply, on the sumptuous bed clothes.

She shook her head. Oliver was so... vital. How could he not be alive? How could she go on without him?

⁂

One day Oliver was fine. The next, he mentioned his head was throbbing and his throat was scratchy but dismissed both as insignificant. His days were busy and long, especially at the moment while France was transitioning to a new king. A headache was a minor, almost predictable consequence, and naught by which to be alarmed.

Unfortunately, this was far more serious than a mere headache. The following morning, Oliver went to work, and tried to continue as normal, but could not summon up the energy, and the embassy sent him home to rest. That evening, he was wracked with fever.

Day and night, Charlotte sat with him, tending to his needs, cooling his hot skin and dosing him with, not only the medications prescribed by the doctor, but also several of her sister-in-law's tried and trusted remedies. The symptoms seemed to ease; Oliver rallied. Then, last afternoon, his condition deteriorated.

Despite Charlotte's diligence, and the efforts of Docteur Allard, the physician assigned to the embassy, Oliver did not respond.

Now he was dead.

⁂

Charlotte was frozen. A hard lump had settled where her heart used to be. She had no idea what to do. Their two children had yet to be told. They knew their Papa was unwell, but everyone was confident he would be up and about by week's end. Charlotte was aware, if she cried, it might help, might alleviate the pain, but she had no tears.

There was much to do... no... none of that mattered today. Today, what was left of it, was for her children, everyone else could wait. Pulling herself together, Charlotte turned away from the spectacular view over the roofs of Paris, a view she barely registered, and retraced her steps across their bedchamber.

Their bedchamber, it was no longer *theirs*, it was hers. Charlotte slumped onto the chair positioned beside the bed, where Oliver lay so still — almost as though in a deep sleep. His body would need to be prepared, but this was France and she was not cognisant of the rules — that Oliver would die on foreign shores never occurred to either of them.

She wanted to take him home to Sherbrooke, their country estate, where he could be buried in the family plot, but was unsure whether transporting a body was permitted or even appropriate. The alternative, to leave him in Paris, among strangers — unconscionable.

Charlotte heaved a sigh and took Oliver's hand. It was cold, but she didn't care. Lifting it, she kissed his knuckles, then held it against her face.

"What do I do? Oliver, what do I do? You weren't supposed to die, to leave me here, alone. How do I go on without you?"

Oliver, of course, didn't respond, but Charlotte could hear his voice in her head.

Charlotte my darling, one thing at a time. First, you must tell the children. They do not need to hear of this from the staff. Noah will try to be brave. I doubt Millie will really understand. I know it will be hard, to explain why I can't play with them anymore, but please just tell them the truth. Don't prevaricate. Children are canny little souls; they know when we are not being honest.

Then write to your mother. I know she will want to be with you, to help you... let her. Permit Donaldson to take care of the rest. Spend time with the children, go for walks, savour the last breath of summer.

Charlotte, I love you. I'm sorry I left you, but please do not waste your life mourning me. Embrace every single moment. I'll find you again... eventually.

Charlotte stretched up and kissed Oliver's cheek. "I'll try my love. I'll try." She leaned back, placed his hand on the bed and patted it, brushing over his long, slender fingers. She always thought Oliver had artist's hands. Hands which, with a simple touch, could calm her or transport her to the heights of bliss. No more.

Standing, she straightened the bed clothes, and stared at her husband for a long moment.

Then, she left the room, closed the door, and went to find Noah and Millie.

The next two weeks passed in a blur. Everything continued around Charlotte, but nothing touched her. Letters were sent to a variety of people. Oliver's secretary and man of business, the aforementioned Donaldson, handled most of them, but Charlotte wrote to her family. Oliver's parents were dead, and he had no siblings, a blessing she did not appreciate until this moment.

Then there was the house, this beautiful house in the centre of Paris where they had been living for the last two years. Rather than rent somewhere, Oliver bought this property, arguing it gave them a home in Paris, even after his appointment with the British Embassy came to an end.

It was a decision neither regretted. They loved the city and were part of a small but close-knit group of friends. Noah, and Millicent — known to all and sundry as Millie — were happy, they had several playmates, and Noah was looking forward to beginning lessons with some of his friends.

Until Oliver's death they had no plans to return to England. Charlotte wasn't ready to leave Paris, *but* she wasn't sure she wanted to bury Oliver here.

In the event, Charlotte arranged for Oliver to be interred at the recently opened *Cimetière des Grandes Carrières* in Montmartre, the eighteenth arrondissement of Paris, and not too far from their home. She did not think it sensible to delay the burial, not least because she had no mind to witness her beloved husband's body begin to decay. The temporary grave marker would be replaced by a tombstone more suited to Oliver's status as soon as it was finished.

The enormity of his loss and the changes it wrought on their lives threatened to overwhelm Charlotte. Her mind refused to settle, questions without answers swirled around her head in chaotic abundance. She lost her appetite and found sleep eluded her. Noah and Millie kept her sane. With the resilience of youth, they cried, talked about what had happened, and moved on.

Seven-year-old Noah understood more than his sister, who had just turned four, although neither of them appeared to be swamped by grief, for which Charlotte was relieved. She had yet to weep for the loss of her husband. She knew she ought to, but was afraid, if she gave in to tears, she would never stop. Thus, even though her control was hanging by the slenderest of threads, she bit her lip... figuratively speaking... and carried on with life as though all was normal.

Her friends were solicitous and, while offering support, were not suffocating in their compassion. Charlotte was appreciative of their sensitivity; it was all she could do to drag herself out of bed each day — to welcome numerous, well-intentioned, callers was beyond her.

Thankfully, being in mourning meant she could avoid all formal engagements for at least six weeks, longer if she felt it appropriate. Charlotte was unsure she would ever attend another ball or soiree again — to go without Oliver? Unthinkable.

Twelve days later, Charlotte was sitting in the garden, watching Noah and Millie, who were playing with two kittens, offspring of the kitchen cat. Their antics were amusing, and Charlotte was amazed to discover she could still smile.

It was mild for October, and Charlotte wanted her children to enjoy as much fresh air as possible. Too soon it would be winter, and outdoor pursuits would be curtailed.

Masson, the butler, came to ask whether she was receiving visitors. Charlotte was about to shake her head when Masson murmured something only she could hear.

Charlotte's mouth fell open.

"Are you sure?" she whispered, not quite believing what he said.

Masson nodded. "*Oui*, my Lady."

Charlotte stood on suddenly unsteady legs and turned to watch as the butler escorted three ladies and one gentleman into the garden. Charlotte did not recognise the latter, but the trio were dearly familiar. Of their own volition her arms lifted, reaching for the oldest of the three.

"Mama," it was a sad lament. The woman enfolded Charlotte in her arms.

"Oh, my poor child."

Finally, the tears flowed.

ABOUT THE AUTHOR

Rosie Chapel lives in Perth, Australia with her hubby and three furkids. When not writing, she loves catching up with friends, burying herself in a book (or three), discovering the wonders of Western Australia, or — and the best — a quiet evening at home with her husband, enjoying a glass of wine and a movie.

Website: www.rosiechapel.com

OTHER BOOKS BY ROSIE CHAPEL

Historical Fiction

The Hannah's Heirloom Sequence

The Pomegranate Tree - Book One

Echoes of Stone and Fire - Book Two

Embers of Destiny - Book Three

Etched in Starlight - Prequel

Hannah's Heirloom Trilogy - Compilation – e-book only

Prelude to Fate

Regency Romances

The Linen and Lace Series

Once Upon An Earl - Book One

To Unlock Her Heart - Book Two

Love on a Winter's Tide - Book Three

A Love Unquenchable - Book Four

A Hidden Rose – Book Five

The Daffodil Garden

The Unconventional Duchess

Rescuing Her Knight

His Fiery Hoyden

A Regency Duet

A Regency Christmas Double

Fate is Curious

HISTORICAL FICTION

The Pomegranate Tree

Hannah's Heirloom - Book One

Hoping to trace the origins of an ancient ruby clasp, a gift from her long dead grandmother, Hannah Wilson travels to the fortress of Masada with her best friend, Max. Strange dreams concerning a rebel ambush begin to haunt Hannah and following a tragic accident, she slips into the world of Ancient Masada.

A woman out of time, Hannah must rely on her instincts and her knowledge of what will befall this citadel to survive. Will she escape, or is she doomed to die along with hundreds of others as Masada falls – and what does any of this have to do with an ancient ruby clasp?

Echoes of Stone and Fire

Hannah's Heirloom - Book Two

Pompeii - a vibrant city lost in time following the AD79 eruption of Vesuvius. Now rediscovered, archaeologists yearn for an opportunity to uncover the town's past. Some things, however, are best left alone - revealing the secrets hidden beneath the stones could prove perilous. Hannah and Max are brought to Pompeii by a surprise invitation to join an excavation team who are trying to uncover the city's long history.

After entering an excavated house that bears a Hebrew inscription, Hannah's two worlds collide, and she falls back through time to ancient Pompeii. A place where her ancestor is a physician to gladiators engaged in mortal combat, where riotous mobs run amok and where a ghost from the past returns to haunt her.

Will Hannah and her loved ones manage to escape the devastation she knows is coming, before the town is engulfed in volcanic ash? Will she ever find her way back to Max the love of her life, waiting not so patiently millennia away? Or will echoes be all that remain?

Embers of Destiny

Hannah's Heirloom - Book Three

AD80 - Hannah and Maxentius must embark on a new journey to Northern Britannia. This harsh frontier is far from the comforts of Rome and danger lurks where least expected; a garrison of soldiers, some unhappy with their isolated posting; local tribes, outwardly accepting of their Roman occupier, but who may still resent the seizure of their lands.

Millennia away, Hannah Vallier finds a familiar item while working in a museum near Hadrian's Wall. It is the pomegranate; carved by Maxentius on Masada. Before Hannah can discuss it with Max, disaster strikes! Believing her husband has been killed, Hannah retreats into the past, her soul melding with that of her ancestor, but with little idea of what they could face. Is the risk from the conquered tribes, or much closer to home?

As rebellion threatens to shatter a fragile peace, Hannah's heart whispers that just maybe Max isn't dead and that he is calling her home. Can she trust her heart, or will she remain caught out of time, her destiny floating away like embers on a breeze?

Etched in Starlight

Hannah's Heirloom - Prequel

Maxentius - a Roman soldier fresh from the battlefields of Armenia, arrives to take command of the military outpost of Masada, Herod's isolated citadel in the Judaean desert. A seemingly mundane posting after years of warfare, Maxentius finds it more challenging to maintain a focused garrison than to face the wrath of the Parthians across a disputed frontier.

Hannah - a young Hebrew physician spends her days dealing with injuries from street brawls, deprivation, disease and loss. As her beloved Jerusalem plunges into chaos; her brother — who belongs to a band of rebels determined to drive out their Roman occupiers — tells her of their plans to storm a desert fortress and steal the weapons stored there, persuading his reluctant sister to go with him.

Masada - following the ambush, Hannah finds and treats three badly wounded Roman soldiers. In the aftermath and against impossible odds, Hannah and Maxentius realise that they are more than healer and captive, their fate already etched in starlight.

❧

Prelude to Fate

For Lucia, staring into the jaws of an horrific death, escape seems impossible.

Rufius Atellus, a veteran Roman soldier, is appalled when he recognises one of the victims about to be executed. Surely this is a ghastly mistake?

A ferocious she-wolf, anticipating a tasty meal, suddenly finds herself under a human's control.

In an unexpected twist, and as danger threatens, the lives of all three become inextricably entwined.

Was it chance brought them together in that theatre of bloodshed, or simply a prelude to fate?

❧

REGENCY ROMANCE

Once Upon An Earl

Linen and Lace - Book One

When Fate saw fit to intervene in the life of Giles Trevallier, the very respectable Earl of Winchester, by dropping a female — soaked to the skin and with no memory of who she is or how she came to be there — literally at his feet, no one could have predicted the outcome.

While uncovering her identity, Giles realises he is falling hopelessly in love with his mystery guest, who unbeknownst to him, is succumbing to similar emotions; but, when the heart is involved, a thoughtless word or gesture can thwart even Fate's best-laid plans.

Faced with misunderstandings, whispers of scandal, secret documents and foreign agents, their chance at a happy ever after seems elusive, but fairy tales often happen when least expected, and love — however inconvenient — usually finds a way to conquer all.

To Unlock Her Heart

Linen and Lace - Book Two

Abused by a duke, and shunned by Society, relief seems at hand when Grace Aldeburgh is bequeathed a house in a small village, far from malicious gossips.

Once there, a tentative friendship blooms between Grace and Theo Elliott, the local doctor, who has already resolved to be the man to unlock her heart.

Just when happiness appears to be within her grasp, her erstwhile tormentor once again stalks Grace. After a failed kidnap attempt, the duke's quest culminates in an acrimonious confrontation, and the reason for his venal pursuit becomes agonisingly clear.

Love on a Winter's Tide

Linen and Lace - Book Three

Every day, Helena disappears into a world few acknowledge, helping the poor, downtrodden, and abused. A husband is the last thing she can be bothered with.

Busy managing his shipping line, Hugh Drummond sees no need for a wife, whose only joy is dancing and frivolity. If — and it was a huge if — he ever married, it would be to a woman as capable as he, not some giddy society Miss.

Then, Hugh meets Helena and despite their resolve, fate, it seems, has other ideas. As their attraction deepens however, treachery threatens to tear them apart. Will they uncover the perpetrator in time, or will their love be swept away, lost forever on a winter's tide?

A Love Unquenchable

Linen and Lace - Book Four

Jessica Drummond, a bright and cheerful young woman, rarely gives romance, let alone love, a thought. Long hours working in her brother's shipping office affords little chance of her ever meeting an eligible bachelor.

Duncan Barrington, veteran of the Napoleonic Wars, believes himself wounded in both body and soul. He has no intention of inflicting his demons on anyone, certainly not a beautiful and, in his opinion, irresponsible city lady.

One cold and snowy morning, the plight of a bedraggled puppy throws Jessica and Duncan together and, as a spark of something indefinable yet wholly unquenchable begins to burn, it is unclear who rescued whom.

A Hidden Rose

Linen and Lace - Book Five

After witnessing his mother's grief at the loss of his father, Nick Drummond resolved never to cause someone he loved such distress. Even the happiness of his siblings would not sway him – until he met Rose.

Rose Archer was almost content assisting her doctor father in a tiny fishing village in the north of Yorkshire. To experience the world beyond, a tantalising dream – until she met Nick.

Unexpectedly, the impossible becomes possible, and the renounced – desired above all things, but the shipwreck that brought them together, may yet tear them apart. Will Nick learn to trust his heart, or will his love for Rose remain forever hidden

The Daffodil Garden

Horrifically scarred during the war, William Harcourt - Marquis of Blackthorne - prefers to spend his days in the quiet of his daffodil garden; plants do not pity, turn away, or judge.

Lucy Truscott, whose life is far removed from that of the *ton*, has no idea that by saving the life of a young woman, to whom she bears an uncanny resemblance, her own will be placed in mortal danger.

A chance encounter leads to something more. William begins to trust that Lucy sees the man beneath the scars, while Lucy is persuaded that love might actually transcend status.

Unfortunately, before their courtship has really begun, someone has every intention of ending it - permanently.

The Unconventional Duchess

Refusing to suffer the humiliation of her husband flaunting his mistress at Society events, the newly married Duchess of

Wallingstead, Ella Lennox, takes control of her life. She leaves London for the family's country seat in remote Yorkshire.

A woman alone, Ella spends the next four years turning a cold, grim house into a home, and transforming the fortunes of the estate. Not afraid of hard work, she soon earns the respect of those around her with her determination and unconventional attitude.

Out of the blue, the duke arrives. Resigned to another arduous visit, Ella is stunned when it seems he is attempting to court her.

Impossible!

Could her dream of a happy marriage be about to come true?

Everything hangs on a snowstorm, a herd of cows and an uninvited guest!

❦

Rescuing Her Knight

The de Wiltons - Book One

A story, invented to keep a little girl distracted, marks the beginning of another tale. One destined to remain unfinished for nearly twenty years.

Against her better judgement, Kitty de Wilton is persuaded to help Adam Marchmain banish his demons. This requires a subterfuge which, if discovered, might shatter more than the bonds of friendship forged two decades previously.

To Kitty, determined to break through the shield Adam has erected, the risk is worth it.

To see his smile and hear his laughter.

To rescue the knight of her childhood.

Just when a fairy tale ending is within her grasp, Kitty is threatened by the man who murdered her husband. In a cruel twist the tables are turned, and Kitty is the one who needs rescuing.

His Fiery Hoyden

A Novella

Livvy has no respect for the nobility; they let her down when she most needed them. Why should she accede to their demands now?

Philip, Lord Harrington, is stunned to discover the young heir to the dukedom lives a stone's throw away in a ramshackle cottage, and resolves to restore the child to his birthright.

They meet in a clash of wills, but just when it seems Livvy might surrender, the victory Philip desires, may not taste all that sweet.

A Regency Duet

Luck be a Pirate

Luck wasn't something retired pirate Kennet Alexson believed in – good or bad. However, even he had to concede that landing a job at Trentams shipyard, and meeting Lynette Collins, was more than coincidence.

Fortune it seemed, was smiling on him for once.

As Kennet adjusts to life on dry land, his friendship with Lynette deepens into something far more enduring, and what once seemed elusive now becomes possible.

Unfortunately, fate has other plans, and Kennet's good luck is about to run out.

The Highwayman's Kiss

Surrendered Hearts – Book One

Nothing exciting had ever happened to Juliette St Clair. Her days were spent assisting her father or calling on friends, wandering art galleries, taking constitutionals or, and more preferably, escaping into her books. Her evenings her evenings — an endless round of balls, where she preferred to remain invisible.

Until the day she was robbed by a highwayman.

A Regency Christmas Double

Heart Rescued

Four years since Jasper lost the woman he was hoping to marry. Four years since he closed his heart and withdrew from Society. He has no idea his reclusive existence is about to be shattered.

Enter his sister's best friend, Harriet, a flame haired beauty, who needs his help.

Reluctantly he agrees and as they spend time together, it is clear their feelings run deep. Although Harriet affects Jasper in a way no woman ever has, he believes her to be out of his league ~ but it's Christmas and she might just be the one to melt his frozen heart

Catch a Snowflake

Romance often blossoms in the most unlikely of places - but in a ward full of wounded soldiers - surely not?

When Lucas Withers comes face to face with Jemima Parsons - a young woman who blames him for her brother's injury - falling in love is the last thing on their minds. What neither of them anticipated, was the magic of snowflakes.

Fate is Curious

A Novella

Happily, ever after? No such thing! Bereft, following her beloved husband's sudden death, Lady Charlotte Sherbrooke has lost her belief in such romantic nonsense.

Successful shipping merchant, Zacharie Romain, is no stranger to loss; his business can be hazardous. Moreover, his wife died in childbirth and even though it happened a decade ago, he has no mind to expose himself to such sorrow again.

They meet in less than joyful circumstances but, as the year turns and grief diminishes, the woes of a small boy become the catalyst for something wholly unexpected. Can Charlotte and Zacharie trust what Fate has in store or will past heartbreak prevent them from taking a chance on love?

A Christmas Prayer

with Ashlee Shades

A Short Story

An entreaty from a frightened child.

Orphaned and only nine, Caroline Thorne has to grow up before her time. She is doing everything she can to keep what is left of her family together and out of the workhouse but is terrified her prayers are not being heard. Or maybe they are…

A petition from a woman desperate for a family.

A chance meeting with three orphaned siblings, tugs at Elizabeth Barrington's heart strings. Thus far, she and her husband have not been blessed with children and, as Christmas approaches, a plan begins to form - one which might just be the answer to her prayers.

Two Christmas prayers, as different as they are the same.

Will they hear and, more importantly, heed the answer?

The Lady's Wager

Surrendered Hearts- Book Two

A Novelette

Ged Mowbray will do anything to avoid being married off to the suitable prospects his parents insist on parading in front of him.

Melissa Bouchard is under no illusion her sizeable dowry is the attraction to suitors, not her.

An overheard conversation leads to an offer too good to refuse, but what happens when a lady's wager, becomes a gamble on the happily ever after, you did not even realise you wanted?

Winning Emma

Surrendered Hearts - Book Three

A Novelette

Randolph Craythorpe — earl, covert operative, and occasional highwayman — believed his dalliance with Lady Felicity Hartwich would lead to marriage. It did, but not to him! The arrival of an unwelcome guest, however, provides the perfect opportunity to indulge in a little retaliation.

Emma Newbury accompanies her cousin, Lady Charity Anscombe, to London for the Christmas season. Once there, she comes face to face with the three men who witnessed the humiliating aftermath of her father's disgrace — one of whom, to her irritation, has taken up residence in her dreams.

Their infrequent encounters only serve to confuse but, while winter tightens its grip on the city, what was inconceivable becomes the one thing for which they both yearn, yet bound by Society's rules, cannot admit.

As the snow falls, Randolph begins to understand that to win Emma, he will have to surrender.

⟡

A Love Impossible

A Regency M/M Novelette

Tasked with investigating a heinous crime, Edward Lindsay travels from London to Dublin — a city which holds too many memories — in the guise of guardian to his sister. He knew it could be hazardous, and relished the challenge, but that wasn't what caused his stomach to tighten as they approached landfall.

Dublin held more than just a murderer.

There was also Aidan.

While attending a party, Aidan Griffen is astonished when he comes face to face with a man who fled Dublin two years previously. A man he has desperately tried to forget.

As Edward closes in on his quarry, a fire, deliberately extinguished, is rekindled. But what of it? Edward and Aidan share a love impossible, and to acknowledge their feelings — more dangerous than confronting a killer.

Is there any hope of a happily ever after?

⟡

Unravelling Roana

A Novelette

Tired of being ignored by her husband, Roana Dumont, Countess of Brooketon does the one thing guaranteed to get his attention. She runs away… to Venice, leaving behind a set of riddles for him to solve… *if* he feels their marriage is worth saving.

Gideon Dumont, 6th Earl of Brooketon is flabbergasted when he discovers his wife has apparently vanished off the face of the earth. A series of puzzles, the only clue as to her whereabouts.

The question is… will he unravel them?

FAIRY TALE ROMANCE

Chasing Bluebells

A Novella

Once upon a time, somewhere in France, there was a man whose reckless obsession led him down a dark path — one which, ultimately, cost him his life. That ought to have been the end of it. Regrettably, as is so often the case, those who least deserve it, suffer for the actions of others.

A decade after being sent away, Sebastien Daviau returns to the little village where everything began. Hoping to lay the ghosts of his childhood to rest, he studiously ignores the possibility, he might run into Charlotte de Montbeliard.

As luck would have it, Charlotte is the one who runs into him... well, his horse... and although the brief encounter leaves a lasting impression, neither recognises the other.

A name revealed causes a freak accident, catapulting Sebastien's past into his present, and bringing him face to face with a man whose reputation would intimidate the most ardent of suitors.

Can whatever is blossoming between Charlotte and Sebastien survive the challenge imposed, or is their happily ever after about to fade as quickly as the bluebells they loved to chase?

CONTEMPORARY ROMANCE

Of Ruins and Romance

Kassandra Winters has intrigued Gabriel St Germain since he accidentally knocked her flying outside her university professor's office. Her face haunts his dreams, yet he never expected to see her again. So, he is surprised when she appears, as though destined to do so, in the middle of a ruin, and he concocts a plan to win her heart.

Gabriel's old-fashioned courtship touches something deep inside Kassie and, although struggling to believe someone as handsome as Gabriel could possibly be interested in her, she soon realises she has fallen irrevocably in love with him. However, just as Kassie shares everything of herself with Gabriel, her world comes crashing down.

Can their romance survive or will it fall in ruins, like the relics of antiquity that brought them together.

All At Once It's You

When Alex arrives in the small village of Rosedale Abbey, to take up a position as a research assistant for a renowned archaeologist, the last thing she is looking for, or expects to find, is love.

Jake was perfectly happy with the status quo. When it came to relationships, he didn't do committed or long term. He called the shots, and if his current flame didn't like it, she knew what to do. A philosophy, which served him well - until he met Alex.

Romance blooms, but even as the untamed wilderness of the North Yorkshire moors weaves its spell, a long-buried secret might yet jeopardise their happily ever after.

Cobweb Dreams

A Novella

A holiday on the Scottish isle of Mull was just the break Chloe Shepherd needed, an escape from her boring office job and her complete lack of anything resembling a social life. Romance, it seems, isn't on the cards and, although Chloe dreams of finding her soulmate she is beginning to believe love is like cobwebs — spun overnight, only to vanish in the early morning breeze.

Under sufferance, Dominic Winters makes a flying visit to Mull to check on a rental property owned by his family. He hasn't got time for this — so indulging in a holiday fling is the last thing on his mind.

A lamb stuck in a bog proves a most unexpected matchmaker and, while Mull weaves its magic, Chloe wonders whether those fragile cobwebs might be far more stubborn than she thought.

Just One Step

A Short Story

In the aftermath of an horrific car accident, Daisy Forrester travels to Italy - hoping, so far from her memories, she might begin to heal.

Archaeologist, and single father, Adam Willoughby is too busy looking after his young daughter to give romance let alone love, a thought.

Neither expects a chance encounter in an ancient ruin to be anything more, but sometimes, that's all it takes.

His Heart's Second Sigh

A Novella

Reuben Faulkner and Paige Latimer are two happily single people, who have no desire to upset the status quo.

Unexpectedly, they are thrown together, only to discover both want far more than a casual friendship.

Just when things take an interesting turn, Reuben's past catches up with them, and threatens to derail their blossoming romance before it has chance to start.